Foreword

Several years ago, a young Egyptian woman appeared at the public library writers group I led. With her kindness and effervescence, she quickly became a beloved member of our group. We had never critiqued the work of an author whose first language isn't English, but we joyfully assisted Rania with her blog posts.

When Rania set out to write a novel in English, I was impressed by her confidence. I was not, however, surprised. Rania's courage led her to write *America Through My Eyes: Experiences of an Egyptian American Muslim Woman* in 2016 in which she shared her firsthand experiences. For her readers, myself included, the book presented an opportunity to grow in understanding and empathy.

With *The Eastwestern Girls*, Rania offers a fictional story of two teens who share similar situations despite geographical and cultural differences. Once again, the reader encounters our common humanity through Rania's insightful narrative.

Jeanne Valentine

Jeanne Valentine served as the adult service manager at Plano Community Library in Illinois for many years, and has been the moderator of the library writers' group since 2007. She is an author who currently lives and writes in Plano, Illinois.

Contents

The Eastwestern Girls

Susan 1
Mark and me

Illinois, USA 2012

I was ready to go back to school after a whole week of being sad and depressed. What happened with my boyfriend was rough. Everyone was telling me that Mark was cheating on me, but I didn't believe anyone until I saw him flirting with a girl last week. I confronted him with what I had heard and he didn't deny it. I didn't know how boys can be okay with doing awful things in relationships. I had to break up with Mark. But it was not easy. He was my first real boyfriend and we were together for seven months, since the beginning of this school year, my junior year in high school. I knew from the beginning he was not the best for me, but I needed a relationship in my life. I actually did that to myself when I liked him and accepted when he asked me out.

After we broke up, I didn't want to go to school, didn't want to see him or anyone who knew what he had done to me. I was so worried about what they would think about me. Maybe they would think I was not good enough for him, so he looked for love with another girl.

But now, I really don't care what they think of me.

I felt better after I convinced myself that everyone knew how bad he was. It was not the first time he'd cheated on a girlfriend and I doubt it will be the last. It was his problem and not mine. I also know not all boys are like Mark. I actually didn't choose well. I was happy that someone liked me and asked me out, so I accepted without really thinking about it.

When I was younger, I found a way to feel better on my rough days. I always imagined another girl the same age, somewhere in the world, going through the same exact problem and who felt the same feelings. We both were sharing what was happening. Thinking that made me feel that I was not alone. That gave me the power and the strength to endure these rough days and get back up. I can do that. All girls can do it, I thought.

I was thinking about that while getting ready for school. I stared at my eyes while finishing the last part of my make-up. Then I looked proudly at my beautiful short red dress on my perfectly shaped body in the mirror, fixed my short blond straight hair and smiled. I grabbed my sweater and snuck out of our small apartment, before my mom or her boyfriend Tommy got up.

In school I walked like an actress on the red carpet, winning an Oscar for the fifth time. I really wanted to show everyone that I had forgotten everything about Mark. I was lucky that I just saw him in one class a day. And I had my plan to totally ignore him.

The first day back at the school went well. I spent most of the time chatting with my best friend Amanda, and I asked her not to talk about anything that would change my good mood. I met Amanda the first time when my mom and I moved to this small town in the suburbs of Chicago when I was in 3rd grade. Since then Amanda has always been my best friend.

From day one, Amanda knew Mark was not the best match for me, but I didn't listen to her. We have to make mistakes in order to learn. As they say, "No pain, no gain." And I gained a lot of experience from everything that happened between Mark and me. From the beginning, he was not serious about me, and I just needed someone to care for me.

Caring! That was all I really needed in my life because I never had someone to care for me. Maybe Amanda was the only one. I was a friend she liked to spend time with, but she definitely cared more about her mom, her dad, her three brothers, and all of her family. Family, and caring. Maybe those are the two things I miss most.

I still remember when I was a little girl living in New York with my mom and her ex-boyfriend, who was my dad. I remember the happy days, but I remember the rough days more. The days my dad used to come home drunk, and how he used to beat my mom for no reason. I remember her crying and her screams for help. I remember myself sitting in the corner shivering, and quietly crying. Scared to do or say anything.

Those days were enough for my mom to hate my dad, and to hate me as well. Maybe because I look a lot like him. We have the same light green eyes, and blond hair. Actually, the only thing I got from my mom was being short.

But I have never been like him in anything other than my looks. He failed at school and I made straight A's every year. He loved alcohol and drugs and I hated them. He hated himself and I love myself and I am proud of who I am. But my mom just judges with her eyes. She doesn't see what's in my heart.

After she was hurt so badly the last time my dad beat her up, she left the apartment and left everything she had there. She left him forever, and took me with her. She said to me one time "If I hadn't left on that day, I would have killed him and would be in prison now." We spent a couple of months homeless. It was such a hard time for us moving halfway across the country until she found a job in a restaurant in this town, rented a small apartment, and we finally have had a quiet decent life since then.

A month after I returned to school after the break-up, I was finally feeling better. I didn't even care if I saw Mark at school. I actually said hi to him and joked with his new girlfriend.

What I was really thinking about on that day was my conversation with Amanda.

"Hey Susan, did you notice Steven?" Amanda asked me during school lunch.

"Which Steven do you mean?"

"Really? You don't know which Steven I'm talking about?" She asked with a knowing look.

"Oh, you mean Steven Johnson," I said with a smile.

"Yes! I'm glad you know which Steven," she said, with the same knowing look, followed by a big smile.

"What do you mean by notice? I think every girl is noticing this Steven every day," I said with a laugh.

"Yes, but he has been looking at you a lot and also he asked me about you." She said, waiting for my reaction.

"Are you serious?" I asked.

"Yes. Totally serious."

Steven Johnson. One of the most handsome and popular seniors at our school. He was one of my favorite types of boys, with his blue eyes, dark straight hair, and fair skin. He had just moved to the area this year, and since his first day, most of the girls in school hung around him. He was tall and muscular, and a very good football player. He also was a smart student, funny, rich, and nice. Who could ask for more! His dad and mom were physicians in town and that was what he was planning to be as well. Steven was a dream I had and never thought it would come true. But now after what Amanda said, it seemed possible, and why not!

Sarah 1
Aunt Fayza

Qena, Egypt 2012

My name is Sarah Alhwary. I was born in Eldweeny, a small village in the city of Qena in Southern Egypt. The big beautiful house I grew up in was the Omdah's or the Mayor's house. My father was the most important man in the village. He became a mayor after his father, who was a mayor after his grandfather, and so on. It was an honor to be a part of this family. Everyone in school and in my neighborhood always looked up to me. Most of them were afraid to be my friends because if we had a problem, I might tell my dad and get them in trouble. Others thought I had a big ego and was not friendly enough to be their friend. The sad part is that I have never done any of that, and I would never want to. I always felt lonely and longed for friends.

My mom died on my third birthday, twelve years ago. My 16th birthday is coming soon, and even though it's not common to celebrate birthdays here in the village, I have my own different celebration on that day, remembering my mom and thinking of her. I don't even remember what she looked like except from some old pictures. But I miss her every day and every time I hear anyone talking about their mother.

I live with my dad, my brother, who is 13 years older than me, and my grandmother, who is my dad's mother and who is the one in control of everything that happens. No one in the house can do anything without her approval, even my dad, the most important man in the village. That is how powerful the old ladies in southern Egypt are.

And then there is my aunt Fayza, the only well-educated one in our house. She is 40 years old and unmarried, not a common thing in our community. Most of the girls in our village marry at a young age, from 15 to early 20s. That is because many girls either don't go to school, or leave school early. But my dad always appreciated education. He only finished high school, but encouraged his sister and his son, and me, to finish college.

My brother hated school and he barely finished a bachelor's degree. He always asked our dad to keep me home, and to accept any of the young men who asked for my hand since becoming a young woman. In contrast, my aunt valued education, and asked my dad to keep me in school, and let me finish my education before marrying.

I have a very special relationship with Aunt Fayza. She is kind, compassionate, and she loves me so much. I've always looked up to her since she is the only one in our village who has a master's degree and even has a PhD in science. She is so smart. She is the only woman in our big family to earn such degrees, and she also works at the university in Qena. That means she has to travel about an hour and half by train to go to work, which she does with passion and love for her career.

My aunt doesn't like the life in downtown Qena, preferring the life in our small village. The cities are so different from the villages here. I feel the opposite of my aunt towards the city and bigger towns. I always dreamed of living in a city where I could see a lot of cars, tall buildings, and many stores. I have been to the city with my aunt and brother to shop and visit fun places many times, and every time I wished to stay there. The bustle, noise mingled with songs, and nice people wearing nice outfits. I can smell life there. The village is very different, very quiet, and darkness is everywhere around as soon as the sun goes down. People in my village wear traditional clothes. The men wear galabiah, which is a long wide plain robe, and they cover their head with a small hat or a turban, while the women mostly wear colorful long wide dresses and scarves on their head. I see green fields everywhere I look. No big buildings. Our house is the biggest of all the buildings there.

I look up to my aunt in everything, except that she is still single at her age. She is well educated and attractive, but she has refused everyone from our village who has asked for her hand. She has always believed they all were asking for her hand because of her family's power, not for herself. Also, she doesn't want to marry a man less educated than her, and most of those who asked for her hand had little or no education. So, she prefers being single and puts up with all the mean comments from our family. She said she would never be able to handle spending her life with someone she didn't want from her heart.

Her heart is another reason for being single. My aunt fell in love with a nice young man at college who had also finished graduate school at the same university. I was young when that happened but my aunt told me all the details. He was kind, handsome, well educated, and from a good family. He loved her and she loved him, but a marriage was impossible. In our culture we shouldn't marry someone from outside the village or at least the city we belong to. It was hard for this man to convince his family who were from Cairo to ask for my aunt's hand in Qena, a distant city, but they finally agreed. When they came to ask for her after traveling eleven hours in the car, the answer from our family was No. Aunt Fayza tried everything to make our family accept him, but she was a failure for the first time in her life.

Sometimes I feel that she refused everyone who asked for her hand after that to punish her family, but she was the one who suffered the most.

Some days I feel guilty when I am grateful that she didn't marry and leave me, or our house. My aunt is the only person in my house who checks on me, helps me with school work, and gives me a hug.

Without her, my life would never be the same.

Susan 2
Mom and me

Illinois, USA 2012

We were living a kind of quiet life for a while, until my mom met Tommy, her current boyfriend. She loved him more than she loved anyone else. She had met him at the restaurant. He was a customer there for years. He used to go to the restaurant with his wife, and my mom was their waitress. One day, when he came into the restaurant, he was sad and told my mom he was going through a divorce. During that, he asked my mom out. My mom didn't take long to think about it. She said yes right away. She didn't even ask me first. She never asked me about any of her other relationships, which always ended with her heart broken. But I really needed her to ask me for this one, at least before she let him live with us.

One day she came back from work with him and said, "Hey Sus, this is my boyfriend Tommy and he's going to live with us." I was angry and yelled at her, but she didn't care, as usual. What made me even angrier was the big smile I saw on Tommy's face in this situation. I really didn't know why she was dealing with me like that all the time. Everything I did to my mom was a reaction to an awful thing she had done to me. But, the worst negative feeling I ever received from her was when I saw the jealousy in her eyes.

What I know about most moms is that they are happy if their kids are good and successful. But my mom was different. She was jealous that I had a perfect shaped body and she was so overweight. She was jealous that unlike her, I always had good grades. She was always jealous when I was happy in a relationship because she was rarely happy with someone. Maybe all of that jealousy came from the hate she had for my dad, but why was she blaming me for things I hadn't done?

I didn't make my mom a failure in school or with men. I also didn't make her gain one hundred pounds in the past eight years. I didn't make her lonely, without any friends or family, and I didn't make her have a hard heart towards her only daughter. I really didn't know whether God made her like that or that was what she had done to herself.

I only remember one long warm conversation with my mom. I was looking for something in the living room, when I found a very old picture in a drawer. I asked my mom about it. She was silent for a minute, looking at the picture, and I saw nostalgia in her eyes, before she told me that picture was of her grandmother and grandfather at their wedding.

"They looked very young in this picture, Mom." I said.

"Yes. My grandmother was 15 years old and my grandfather was 16," she said.

"Really!! How did they marry young?" I asked.

"People back then used to marry young. There was no other way to have a relationship with each other," she said.

"What do you mean? They wouldn't live with each other for a while before marriage?" I asked.

"Nope, they wouldn't," she answered.

"But why? I can't even imagine getting married to someone I don't know well, and I haven't lived with for a while."

"Most people back then were religious," she said.

"What do you mean? I see religious people live together without being married!"

"OK. I have to explain this better to you. In Christianity, a man and a woman shouldn't sleep with each other without being married. It is considered a sin, so anyone unmarried wouldn't have a full relationship until marriage. And most of the society was like that. It was part of the culture back then. But it's different now."

"But I have heard it is a crime now to marry young. Is that right?" I wondered.

"I heard on T.V. Once, here in Illinois, the minimum age is 18 for both boys and girls. But in other states people can legally marry younger," she said.

"Really! Do you know what state has the youngest minimum age?"

"I searched for that when I was with your dad in high school. I really wanted to marry him back then. I found out Massachusetts had the lowest age with parental consent, 14 years old for boys and 12 for girls. We couldn't move there and marry because our parents wouldn't allow that to happen, and thank goodness it didn't."

I knew the conversation might turn bad because of the mention of my dad, so I switched the subject back to the picture.

"This picture is really beautiful, and I know you loved your grandmother," I tried to keep her in a good mood; we rarely had a good conversation like that one.

"Yes. I loved her so much and I really wish I could see her."

"I didn't know she was still alive. Where does she live now, and why don't you visit her or call her?" I asked.

"My grandmother was diagnosed with Alzheimer's about ten years ago. My mom was the youngest of her nine children. Grandma told her that she had her when she was 45 years old. Later in my mom's life she knew that she was not her daughter, but her granddaughter. My mom's real mom was her older sister. But my grandmother hid the truth because her daughter got pregnant outside of a marriage, and it was shameful as I told you, so she told everyone the baby was hers. I think that was the reason my mom wasn't able to have a good relationship with any member of her family. She met my dad when she was 14. She had me when she was 15," she said sadly.

Then my mom continued, "she was afraid to tell her family about her pregnancy because it was still shameful to get pregnant that young and unmarried, so she ran off with my dad to a different state. They lived together for seven years and then they married."

"Is 15 the same age you had me, Mom?" I wondered.

"No. I had you when I was 17," she said.

"Were your parents ever okay with you being pregnant at 17?" I asked.

"I know this might sound like a curse in my family, which hopefully won't happen to you, or I will kick you out of my house forever." She stared at me for warning.

"What curse?" I asked.

"To have a relationship with someone, when your parents are against it. My parents didn't accept my relationship with your dad from the beginning. But unfortunately, I didn't listen to them and stayed with him. We found jobs, rented a room in a house and lived together there until we had you. When you were just a year old, he became addicted to drugs, and my life became hell." Mom was sad now.

I had unintentionally switched the conversation back to my dad and the dark days. I realized this when she suddenly started yelling at me for wasting her time.

Though this conversation ended with yelling, it was the best I have ever had with my mom. It was the first time she ever shared some memories and feelings with me. It was my first time seeing her from the inside. She wished for me to escape her family's curse. I had learned a lot about her family and for the first time, I discovered some kindness lived in her tough heart.

Sarah 2
The unknown

Qena, Egypt 2012

In my beautiful spacious room with its classic oak furniture rarely found in a small village like ours. I got up from my four-poster dark brown bed, moved to my big oak dresser chest, looked in the batwing mirror and thought, *my eyes are really pretty*. At my school, the girls always admired my nice eyes. My grandmother told me that my eyes looked exactly like my mom's. Big black eyes with long thick eyelashes. My long wavy black hair and tall body are also like my mom's. My dad told me that my mom left him when she died, but she left him an image of hers, me.

I always wished I had lighter skin like girls from north Egypt, or fair skin, like girls I see in western movies, but then I think my tan skin matches my eyes and hair perfectly, and that's better. It is my second year of high school. Our village has separate schools for girls and boys. One more year and I will be done with high school. I can't wait to finish and go to college, not just because I will see boys there, but also because I want to study history and be a history teacher.

Sarah 2

History has always been my favorite subject. I enjoy listening to stories, and that is why I really love history. The idea that I would go into town for college gave me a chill of happiness. Hopefully I would meet a nice handsome young man there who would fall in love with me and marry me. But I would make sure he was from our village, or at least the town, so my family would not refuse him, like what had happened with my aunt.

One day, I put on my school uniform, a long navy-blue skirt, a white long-sleeve shirt, black shoes, and my white scarf. I had covered my hair and my body, a practice we call hijab, since I was twelve years old. I didn't decide for myself to do that. All the girls in our small village were expected to do that or be considered odd. Sometimes I look at my beautiful hair before I cover it and wish that I was born in the city or even in a different country so I wouldn't have to cover it, or choose when to do it. But at least all the girls in my school are covering their hair like me.

It was a beautiful sunny day in October. We all got up early that day for work and school which rarely happens. I ate breakfast with my dad, my brother, and aunt for the first time in a while. Then, I left for school. On my 20 minute walk to school, I passed a sugarcane field and railroad. I always left around 6:30 a.m. so I had enough time to cross the railroad track before the 7 a.m. train. The sound of trains has always scared me. When I hear it, I feel like I would miss something or someone. And I didn't know why I always had felt that way.

Leaving, and passing the roads and the railroad tracks before hearing the sound at 7 a.m. was a sign of a good day. If I was late, the sound signaled a bad day. This thought was enough for me to leave on time every day.

I wished I had a twin. The idea of another girl who looks exactly like me and shares everything with me, even my mom's womb, would be amazing to me. I would share my thoughts with her, my fears, my problems, my hopes, and my walks to school. I always walked to school alone. Sometimes, I sang on my way, and other times I talked to myself. I asked myself questions and answered them, or imagined stories, which might have happened in the places I pass on my way, hundreds of years ago or thousands of years ago. My walks to school were enjoyable, because I always kept myself entertained.

Sometimes I see girls walking in groups to school, and many times I think about starting a conversation with them. Maybe we could be friends and walk together, but I never had the courage to do so. I always was afraid they would refuse me or leave me after they realized my dad's position, as happened before with a friend from 6th grade. I didn't want to risk any disappointment. I live in peace with no friends, no drama, and no jealousy.

As I passed the sugarcane field that day, I felt like someone was walking behind me. I looked back, but I couldn't see anyone. I kept walking. Five minutes later, I had the same feeling returned, but no one was there when I looked back. I thought maybe it was only a stray animal, a cat or a dog, but I felt scared, so I started running to cross the railroad tracks fast, and get into my school, which was a couple minutes past the tracks. Finally, I reached the school safely, and there I took a deep breath.

Susan 3
Tommy and me

Illinois, USA 2012

Everything in my life was going fine until that day when Tommy joined our life. I never felt comfortable around him. His look toward me always gave me the creeps. That was just an unpleasant feeling, until one awful night.

I was asleep for the night when I woke to a sound in my bedroom. I was scared and turned on the light next to my bed. Tommy was sneaking toward me. I was shocked and yelled at him, "What are you doing here?"

"Don't scream," he said. He put his hand over my mouth. "Susan, be quiet and listen to me. I'm here because I really like you, from the first second I saw you."

"You're a crazy jerk and a cheater. Get out of here right now or I'll call out to my mom, and tell her everything you just said."

"That's fine. Tell her anything, and I will too." He moved back toward the door.

I was shivering. "What do you mean?"

"If you tell her I came here, I'll tell her you called me to your room and when I refused to do what you wanted, you acted like a victim. Let's see who she believes, you or me." He said this with a big smirk as he leered at me.

I jumped out of bed in a rage and shoved him out of the room while cursing at him. At that moment, I didn't really care if my mom heard me. All I was feeling was so much hatred for Tommy. I had to get him out of my room and out of our lives if I could.

I wished I'd never have to see him again. But sadly, I had to see him the next morning and act like nothing had happened at night, because unfortunately, he was right in everything he said. My mom would not believe me if I told her what happened. Her love for him, and her need for him in her life, was more than any good feeling she had for me.

I didn't have a choice but to deal with this awful person every day, and the only thing I could do to protect myself was to lock my bedroom door every single night.

My life became harder after that incident. I tried to limit my time at home, and my time around Tommy and my mom. I was more stressed than ever before. Keeping my grades up at school was not as easy. But school was my only escape. I had to create a good future for myself.

My dream was to be a journalist. I loved writing and reporting, and being a journalist didn't require as many years of college. Graduating with a bachelor's degree in journalism would be enough to start a career. If I were lucky, I might find a job with a big magazine or television network. Then my income would be enough to pay back the college loan and live a good life. I also really wanted to travel all over the world, especially to Greece, Egypt, and Italy, where the world had the greatest ancient civilizations.

These dreams might be hard to achieve, but who knew what my future would hold. First, I had to finish high school and find a way out of this scary house. Yes, I had to leave any way I could, and as soon as I could.

Sarah 3
The first glance

Qena, Egypt 2012

I spent my school day with 45 other classmates in my small classroom at the old building, which was built about 30 years ago. I know 45 sounds like a lot, especially since our classroom is not big, but other schools in bigger cities have more students in each class. The reason we have that many students in a small room is that our village has the only high school for five small villages. I feel lucky I live in this village and I don't have to travel far to school every day.

In the class, six students sit shoulder to shoulder at each desk, which should take three students. It is uncomfortable, but I am lucky to be the Omda's daughter so, every school year, the principal makes sure I sit in the front of the class with fewer students at my desk.

On this day, at school, I had a normal, very boring and uncomfortable day. We never have any fun classes, activities, music or library. The teachers never make learning enjoyable. We just listen to information and lectures all day. When I asked my teacher why we never had music or library, she said the school couldn't afford enough teachers, so they had to eliminate some subjects. And they considered all the fun classes unimportant. Gym and art were not included in the grades earned, so neither the teachers nor the students cared about gym and art. We spent these two classes chatting with each other, mostly TV shows or about our favorite singers and actors. I always chatted with Mariam, my Christian friend who was one of the nicest girls in my class.

"Something weird happened to me this morning on my way to school," I said. "I felt like someone was following me, but every time I looked back to check, I didn't see anyone."

"Maybe it was your imagination?"

"No, I am not crazy." I was annoyed by that question.

"OK, if you didn't watch a scary movie last night, it might be an animal, our village is safe." she said, "I don't think it was someone following you to hurt you."

"I know. That is why I feel confused about it."

"If you are scared, you can ask your dad to assign you a guard to keep you safe," she said.

"No. I don't think I will tell my dad anything," I said.

"Maybe it was an animal like you said. But if it happens again, I might tell him."

"That makes sense. If I was living close to you, I would go with you, but you know I live in the west village."

"Yes. I understand, Mariam. Don't worry. I will be okay."I was trying to act strong but, deep in my heart, I was scared to go back home alone.

I heard the bell that announced the end of the school day.

"Hey, school is done," I said pointing to the young man with the charcoal grill. "Do you want to join me for grilled corn again?"

"I am so happy someone is selling grilled corn around here." she said smiling. "You know I love it, and would never say no to having some, but you will have to pay as usual."

"Yes, I will."

We both headed towards the guy.

"Alsalamu Alikum, we need two soft grilled corn, please!" I said.

"Walikum Assalam, sure, I have the best two ears of corn ready for you," he said, handing me two blackish grilled ears of corn served nicely on the husks, and decorated with the silk.

"What? For me?" I asked, looking at his face for the first time. "How did you know I would buy some today?"

"You and your friend bought from me twice last week, and this week you bought once, so I expected that you would come before the end of the week."

"Oh, do you count how many times all your customers buy from you?" I asked.

"No, not all of them, just the important ones," he said.

I had a weird feeling when he looked into my eyes saying these words. I wasn't sure what he meant. But I had a feeling I had known him before. I also felt there was something I liked in his beautiful hazel eyes. I realized I had seen him selling corn close to our house. I took the two ears of corn, paid my money, and walked back to my friend who was waiting a couple steps away.

"This is so yummy!" Mariam said, after taking a big bite from the corncob. "Sarah, are you OK? Why are you staring into space and not eating your corn?"

"I am fine," I said. I was eating my corn, but sneaking looks at the tall handsome young man, with his medium dark skin and black curly hair. He was staring at me at the same moment.

I went back home that day thinking of everything that young man said. I totally forgot about the fear from the morning. I didn't even wonder whether someone was following me back home.

When I reached my house, I went directly to my room. Later on that day I saw my aunt. I wasn't sure if I should tell her about my day, but I decided to ask her about the corn boy. She knows a lot more than I do about the people in our village. I decided not to tell her about the suspicion of someone following me. If she felt I might be in danger, she would tell my dad, and I really didn't want my dad to assign a guard for me. I didn't want the girls in school to talk about that, and it might keep them further away from me.

"Hey, Aunt Fayza, do you have time now to talk?"

"Sure, Sweetie, what's up?" she said.

"Something happened today and I want to tell you about it."

"What happened? Let me guess if it was good or bad." She was staring at me to see any sign.

"Neither, I just need to ask you about something,"

"OK. What thing?"

"I don't want to talk here. Can we go to my room? I don't want anyone to hear me."

"Let's go," she said.

We went into my room. I sat on the bed and she sat on the chair across from me.

"What happened? You are making me worried," she said.

"Don't worry. Do you remember the young man who used to sell corn at the end of our street a while ago?"

"Do you mean Sileem? Ali's son?"

"Do you know him?" I asked.

"I know he is the son of Ali, our farm guard," she said.

"Our farm that's behind our house?"

"Yes."

"But how come I see Ali, but I have never seen his son around here before?" I asked.

"Because his son doesn't live here with him. He lives with his grandmother on the other side of the village. I am not sure why, but I think it is because he goes to the trade school there. His dad told me that he sells corn after school every day to support his big family. Ali has eight children, and I think Sileem is the oldest."

"That makes sense!" I said.

"Did he bother you or say something he shouldn't say?"

"Not at all. He didn't do anything. I was buying some corn from him today and I had a feeling he knew me, and that was a little weird since I didn't remember I had met him before. But later I remembered he sold corn on our street."

"Well. I have another story about him, but I am sure you don't remember it. He used to play with you in the front yard when you both were young."

"Really!"

"Yes. When your mom died, my brother wasn't really paying attention to anyone or anything. I felt bad for you because you lost your mother at such a young age, and you were a very lonely child. When I saw that little boy who was a couple years older than you playing in the front yard while his dad was working, I let you play with him. But after a couple of months, when your dad realized that, he was very angry. He yelled at Ali for letting his son play with you, and he asked me not to let that happen anymore."

"Oh, I don't remember any of that."

"It is an old story and I don't expect either of you to remember it. Anyway, if he does anything he shouldn't do, let me know and I will take care of it."

"OK. I will let you know. Thanks Auntie!"

"You're welcome. How is school?" she asked.

"Fine, I am doing well this year."

"Are you still planning to be a history teacher?"

"Yes, and I still get my best grade in history."

"I was hoping you'd change your ambition to science."

"No way, Auntie! Science is impossible for me. You know, I love you but hate science."

"OK. I have to go do some work for tomorrow. And I want you to finish your homework and study until it's time for dinner."

"Sure, Auntie. I will"

She left the room, and I lay down on my bed, staring at the ceiling and thinking of everything that happened that day, especially Sileem's words and eyes.

Susan 4
Steven and me

Illinois, USA 2012

I was sitting at the lunch table at school with my friends Amanda and Noah, when Steven walked toward our table. He looked directly into my eyes. He greeted us; Amanda and Noah greeted him back.

"Do you mind, guys, if I sit with you?" he said, maintaining eye contact with me.

"Sure, you can join us," said Noah.

"I wasn't sure if Susan wanted me here. She didn't even say Hi back," he said with a playful grin.

"Sure, you're welcome to hang out with us anytime, Steven," I said.

He sat down next to me.

"I wasn't sure if you were okay with being friends with me."

"I never had a chance to talk with you; maybe because we are not in any class together, but that doesn't mean I don't want to be your friend. I think a lot of people in school would like to be your friend." I said.

"Really! Why do you think so?"

"Hmmm! Maybe because you are a nice person!"

"Do you think that is the only reason?" he said.

"Are you waiting for a specific answer from me?" I said, happy, and nervous at the same time.

"No, saying I'm nice is enough for me today." He started eating his sandwich.

Amanda and Noah joined the conversation until the bell rang. Then we each went to our own classes.

I went home in a very good mood. I couldn't sleep at all that night. I couldn't really believe that Steven seemed interested in being my friend. Amanda called me at least five times. I knew she wanted to talk to me about his conversation, but I didn't want to talk about it at all. I didn't want to feel like he really liked me, and then it may end up with us just being regular friends. I knew he didn't have a girlfriend, but that wasn't enough to give me hope. We always questioned why he didn't have a girlfriend since most of the girls in school dreamed of being with him, but I didn't care about answering that question now. All I cared about was the possibility of me being his girlfriend.

The next day, Steven joined us again at lunch. And he kept joining us every day for a whole month. Everyone at school was talking about the attention he was giving me. I actually noticed a couple of girls pointing at me in the hallway, and I had no doubt that was what they were talking about. Even though he didn't say anything directly yet, the way he looked at me, sat next to me, and offered to help me with schoolwork; all were signs of something to come.

"Hey Susan," said Amanda. "I noticed Steven was talking with you yesterday after school and you seemed happy. Has he asked you out yet?"

"No. I actually don't know what he's waiting for. We keep talking for hours in school and after school. He is acting like he likes me. Everyone is talking about a relationship between us. I always try to show that I'm interested in him, but he still hasn't asked me out."

"Maybe he is reluctant to ask you out since he's a senior and you're a sophomore. Maybe he thinks your mom won't agree?"

"But many seniors date younger girls. I don't think my mom would really care how old my boyfriend is. She has never even asked me if I have a boyfriend. I dated Mark for seven months and broke up with him, and she had no idea about anything. I told her once that we were going to have a sleepover at a friend's house on the weekend, and she didn't bother to ask if I had a boyfriend who would be there with me."

"Yes," Amanda said. "But don't forget, Steven doesn't know anything about all of that. So, he might be nervous asking you out."

"What do you think I should do?" I asked.

"I think you should share that with him."

"What? Do you want me to say that my mom doesn't care about me, or about who I'm dating, so you can ask me out, Steven? I would never do that."

"I didn't say that exactly," she said. "I just want you to give him the green light before any of the other girls get him,"

I thought about everything she said. Just thinking that he might not be my boyfriend was driving me crazy, especially since we had already gotten closer to each other recently. I really liked him. He was everything I wished for. He might be the savior of my rough life. I had to do anything I could to keep him for myself.

The next morning, Steven walked into the school.

"Hey, Steven. How are you today?"

"I'm fine,"he said, smiling. "I can't wait for summer break,"

"Me too. When is your birthday?"

"On May 12, I'll be 18. And you?" That was the question I expected him to ask.

"I will be 16 in two weeks."

"Oh! It's coming soon. I am glad I asked then."

I really wished I was older than 16. That would make it easier for him to take a step. I liked him so much. I thought the coming weeks would make my relationship with him clear. Either we would be together or not.

After that, we talked almost every day, and we met each other in school and outside. We shared many stories. I told him everything about myself, my mom, and even about Tommy. I have never felt comfortable with someone like I have felt with him.

He also told me about his family, but not much. He told me his parents always had high expectations of him and they cared a lot about his future. They were planning for him to be a physician like them, and the cost of college wouldn't be any problem for them since they don't mind spending any amount of money for their child's future.

Two weeks after this conversation, what I really wished for happened. Steven sent me a text to meet him after school in the small café in town. I wore a fancy red tank top and my black shorts. I spent an hour curling my short blond hair. I was so happy. I was expecting a birthday gift from him, but what I didn't expect was that he would ask me out on the same day. But he also asked me for something on that day, and that was unexpected.

"You know, I liked you from the first time I saw you, Susan."

"Me too," I replied, somewhat flustered.

"I also wished you would try to talk with me or get closer to me, as most girls in the school do. But that didn't happen. I waited for a while after you broke up with Mark, then I decided I had to do it myself. And I am so happy now that you like me as well, and want to be with me. I just have one request from you."

"What's that?"

"You know I am almost two years older than you, and my dad is a very important doctor. Also, he is planning to run for Congress. My parents wouldn't really approve of our relationship, because of the age difference and the timing."

"What do you mean about timing?" I asked.

"My parents won't mind me dating in general but, as I told you, they are busy planning for my dad's future and all they want for me now is to get good grades this year. And starting a relationship with a sophomore at the end of my senior year won't make them happy, for sure."

"OK. But our friends are already noticing there is something between us, Steven."

"That's different from confirming it," he said.

"So, you don't want me to tell anyone that you asked me out, and that we are dating each other?" I was so angry.

"Right. No one should know anything about it for a while." He stated this sternly with a calm voice.

"What do you mean *for a while?*"

"I mean we can date secretly for now, and when I go to college and you turn 18, we will be free to do whatever we want to do together and then we will let everyone know about our relationship," he explained.

"But I can't keep my feelings secret as if I'm doing something wrong." I felt the tenseness in my muscles and the dryness in my mouth.

"Babe, listen to me. I love you and want to be with you, not just now, but maybe for the rest of my life. What I am asking you to do now is the best for both of us. Believe me, Susan. This is my first and only request to be with you," he said with the same steady tone.

"But I can tell my mom, right?"

"No, hon, no one should know, especially your mom. You told me she doesn't like you, and that means she might do something to come between us. Also, the age issue would give her a way to do that. I can't risk that with everything I told you."

"I don't know what to say, Steven!"

"Don't say anything now. Take your time to think about it, and I will accept anything you choose. We either would be together secretly for a while or not at all." He kissed my hand, and left his gift on the table.

I looked at his empty chair for a couple of minutes, then I decided to open the gift and see what he got me. I was stunned; I saw a beautiful necklace in the box. My jaw dropped. I had never worn something as beautiful and expensive as this necklace. I had many mixed feelings at that moment: stunned, happy, angry, worried, and confused.

I went home carrying all those heavy feelings. I went directly to my room, closed the door behind me, and laid down on my bed. Took a deep breath, and thought of everything that had happened with Steven. The way he looked at me and the lovely words he spoke were unbelievable. I couldn't believe my ears and eyes.

I closed my eyes and imagined my life with him. I actually imagined myself wearing a beautiful white wedding dress and him standing next to me in a sharp black tux. Everyone we knew was around, us happy and excited. Even my mom, who I thought would be jealous of me on a day like that, was happy for me. I imagined the people calling me Mrs. Johnson. Would that daydream come true one day? I didn't know, but I knew if I refused his only request, it would never happen. I really wished I could show the girls how he chose me, but the weight of his request dismissed those thoughts. I had wished to be with him everywhere and anytime, but now it seemed like I had to sacrifice some of my dreams for a time. He promised he'd tell everyone everything when he could, and one year or a little more was not that long. It was weird that it didn't take me that long to agree to his request. I really loved him, and he was my only way to get out of this home. I also needed some excitement in my boring life, and this year with Steve, we could make the most exciting memories together.

Susan 4

I sat up when I heard my phone ring, thinking it might be Steven. I picked up the phone quickly and saw Amanda's name on it.

"Hey Sue, the birthday girl! Where have you been? she asked "I thought you were coming to the soccer game at school today. I was hoping to see you there to give you the birthday gift which I forgot to give you at school."

"I'm sorry, Amanda, I didn't feel good after school today, so I rested at home."

That was my first lie to Amanda ever. I always told her everything, and I didn't know whether I could keep lying to her for a whole year.

"No problem," she said, "take good care of yourself and hopefully I'll see you tomorrow at school."

The next day, I didn't see Steven. I looked for him everywhere but couldn't find him. I asked his friends, and they told me he hadn't come to school that day. I was hoping he would call me to ask about my decision, but he didn't. I got my phone out to call him but I decided at the last second not to do it.

I can wait until he calls.

Three days passed, and Steven didn't try to see me, call me, or even say hi. He intentionally ignored me and that drove me crazy. I didn't know why he did that. Did he change his mind and not want to date me anymore? Did he go through a hard time with something I didn't know about?

It didn't seem like he was just trying to give me time to think about what he told me. And if so, why was he totally ignoring me?

I missed him so much, his company, his caring, our long chats and phone calls at night. Finally, I decided to call him and tell him that I agreed to his request to be with him. I picked up my phone and called him, but he didn't answer.

I was so disappointed and wondered why.

Sarah 4
Fear and joy

Qena, Egypt 2012

I got scared again, in the morning, feeling someone had followed me. I thought many times about telling my dad, but I always changed my mind, because having a guard with me every day would be worse than this.

If the person wanted to hurt me, I would have been killed by now. And if they were doing that to scare me, I should be strong enough to not be scared.

That was how I convinced myself to walk to school every morning, when my knees were sometimes shaking in fear.

These were my mornings before school, but in contrast, I always looked forward to my after-school time. Not just the fun of chatting with Mariam, but also that thing that led me to buy corn from Sileem every single day. I wasn't sure whether I was trying to help him because I knew that he was supporting his big poor family, or because I really liked the comments he always made when he saw me. Or maybe I liked the joy I felt through the amazing looks I saw in his beautiful eyes. So, I just bought corn every day.

"Hey Mariam, do you want corn today?"

"No. I'm sick of eating corn, Sarah. What about cotton candy today?"

"Mmm, I'm okay with cotton candy, but I'll buy an ear of corn for later."

"Really?" she wondered. "Why do you keep buying corn every day now?"

Her question scared me for a second. I was afraid she understood the real reason. "No reason, except I read about how good corn is for you, so I decided to get one every day."

"What? Corn is not that good for you. You actually could gain weight from an ear of corn every day, believe me." She winked, which scared me more.

After my conversation with Mariam, I stopped getting corn from Sileem for a whole week. I decided not to get corn again until she would ask me for corn. But I couldn't stop myself from stealing looks at him and getting smiles from him every day after school. I felt some fear going to school in the morning, and I felt fun and happiness every day after school seeing him around and looking at his eyes.

Until that day!

I finished school and was looking forward to seeing the cute corn boy as usual. I looked around everywhere, but I didn't see him or his grill. I lowered my head down, kicked a small rock on the ground as far as I could with disappointment. I also was worried. What happened to him, and why was he not there? Was he sick? Is he coming back or did he find another place to sell his corn? Will I see him again or will he be gone forever? All these questions were jumbled in my mind with no answers.

Maybe he will be back tomorrow. I just need to wait. I told myself that, but I was acting weird. I didn't want to chat with Mariam as I used to do every day after school. All I wanted to do was to go home and be alone in my room.

I felt the fear in the mornings but missed the joy in the afternoons.

The next morning, I got myself ready and had made a decision, that if I felt I was followed again, I would tell my dad. I was sick of being worried and, no matter what would happen with a guard walking with me every day, at least I wouldn't be scared. But unexpectedly I had a good quiet walk to school in the morning. I wished I could have a nice after-school time eating an ear of corn. That would be a perfect day, since I had a nice walk to school.

But after school, again I didn't see him. When I saw his empty spot that emptiness filled my heart. I really didn't know why. I didn't even know him well enough to have any real feelings for him. I never felt that towards anyone before. I asked myself, was it because of what my aunt told me about him playing with me or about him helping his family? The answers were no, because he was not the only one who helped his family and I didn't even remember him playing with me when we were little children. Then why was I worried about his absence and why did I need to see him so much? I had no idea! I stood in front of my school and looked at his spot. I walked to his spot and stood at it, then I looked everywhere, hoping to see him in a different place but, filled with disappointment, I left.

For the first time, on my way back home, I felt like someone was behind me; my heart raced and I started to walk faster and faster. I looked behind and started to run, hoping to reach my home quickly to tell my dad about it. Suddenly, someone jumped out in front of me, and I screamed. I looked at that person's face and it was Sileem, the corn boy, my joy. I couldn't believe my eyes and I was scared, happy, and shocked at the same time.

"Calm down! I am so sorry if I scared you!" Sileem said.

"What are you doing here and why are you following me? Have you been following me all that time?" I said in one breath.

"OK. I will tell you everything you need to know, but I want you to calm down first."

"No, you will tell me now!" I said with a louder voice, stomping my feet on the pavement.

"OK. Yes. I was following you as much as I could in the morning to school, and every time you looked back, I was hiding in the fields," he said.

"Why?" I asked.

"The answer is long and I know you can't be late getting home. You can go home now, and I will meet you tomorrow right after school on the back road so it will be easier to talk without anyone seeing us. I don't want to be the reason for any trouble for you, Sarah."

"And why on earth do you think I will meet you where no one can see us?"

"Because I saw you looking for me after school today and I know you want to know all the answers. And I really want you to know it as well." He was looking with his beautiful eyes directly into mine.

"For your information, I was looking to get corn, not for any other reason. And I want to know the answers, but I will not see you tomorrow anywhere. If you ever try to follow me again, I will tell my dad. Do you understand?" I was trying to resist the attraction I felt when he was talking. Then I turned away, left him and ran home. On my way, I was trying to keep myself from looking back, into his eyes, one more time.

I got back home, and couldn't believe what had happened. The one who scared me all these days was the same person I felt happy being next to for a few minutes every day!

I knew what I told him was the right thing to say, but in my heart, I really wanted to see him tomorrow and sit next to him, look at his eyes and listen to all his answers about my questions. But this seemed impossible. If anyone would see us sitting together in the field and tell my dad, it would be the end of the world. I would be in bad trouble. Also, it would bring shame to my dad and my whole family, according to our village traditions. I really didn't want to be the reason for my dad's shame. I loved my dad, even if I felt sometimes that he loved his work, his power, and his money more than me. But in my heart, I knew that I was important to him.

I thought about telling my aunt what happened, but I quickly decided not to. She would never keep it a secret; she would tell my dad or my brother, or would ask me to promise I would never talk with him again, to protect me.

While eating dinner with the family that night, I thought, *no one would trust that I can protect myself and that I am old enough to do the right thing.*

When it was time for bed, I was thinking about the next day. Would he come to sell corn again in the same place? Would he follow me again? Would he try to speak to me again after school? I really wanted to see him at the place he asked to meet me at, but I closed my eyes to sleep, making myself a promise that I would not be able to keep.

I have to not see Sileem or talk to him again.

Susan 5
The lie

Illinois, USA 2012

After those three days of waiting, I was full of happiness when I opened my eyes in the morning to my phone ringing and saw Steven's name on the phone screen. Finally, he was calling me.

"Good morning, my princess."

"Really! I'm a princess?"

"Sure. Not just a princess, but the most beautiful princess ever."

"I almost didn't answer since you didn't answer my calls."

"I don't believe it. You'll always answer my calls right away."

"Is this extreme confidence?" I asked, smiling.

"No, it's extreme love that I know you have for me, and you know I have for you."

I couldn't respond to his words. I felt like flying. I wanted to shout yes, I love you! But I knew I couldn't let anyone around hear me, so I was back to earth.

"You know me well, Steve."

Steve and I spent time together almost every day for the next month. We met in cafes outside town. He brought me valuable gifts, said the best words ever to me, and listened to everything I said. We liked the same kind of music, hip-hop. We both loved action movies. I found in him a brother, a father, a friend and my future lover. He was the best match for me and he became everything to me. I used my home just for sleeping, which made my mom happy. She saved money on food and she had more time to spend with her Tommy.

My friendship with Amanda was not like before. I had to limit my time and my conversations with her. And that was not easy.

At the end of that wonderful month, Steven took me on a car ride and asked me for one more thing. "Do you want to party together this weekend?"

"What do you mean? You, me, and our friends?"

"No. Just me and you!"

"How will we party alone, and where?"

"I'll show you, and it will be in a very special place."

"What place?"

"My grandfather used to live in this town a long time ago, and he had a very old house north of here. I got the key and we can party together there this weekend. What do you think?"

"Steve, you know I would love to spend time with you, but what should I tell my mom?"

"Sue, you said that your mom doesn't mind if you sleep over with friends, so it shouldn't be a big deal."

"But I always tell her where I'm going and she knows all my friends in the area. What should I tell her now?"

He stopped the car in a parking lot, looked into my eyes and held my hand. "You can tell her anything. I don't think she will check if you are lying or not. Let's do it. Babe."

At that moment, I couldn't say no to him. I couldn't resist the love I felt coming from his beautiful eyes. "OK, Steve, I'll find a way to be with you this weekend."

"I knew you wouldn't let me down."

He gave me a kiss before he drove away.

The next day, I stayed home after school, waiting for my mom to come back from work. I also planned to eat dinner with her and Tommy that night for the first time in a while.

"Hey, Tommy, is Mom back yet?" I asked.

"Not yet. Do you need anything?" he said, looking at me with lust.

"I will never need anything from you. You know, I really hate you, Tommy."

"Fine. I was just checking," he said.

Then my mom opened the door, carrying a big box of pizza from where she worked.

"Hey, Mom, how are you?"

"You're not locked in your room or out with your friends. Is everything okay?"

"Yeah, everything is fine," I said. "I just want to let you know that I'm going to a party with my friends this weekend."

"A sleep-over party?" she asked.

"Yes," I tried to avoid looking at her eyes.

"Amanda's house like last time?"

"Yes, she invited me today."

"That's fine, but make sure there are no boys there," she said. She sat down, opened the box of pizza and started eating. Tommy sat next to her and took a big bite, like a pig that hadn't eaten for days.

"Aren't you eating with us?" Tommy asked.

"OK, sure." I sat across from them. I ate a piece of pizza while trying not to look at my mom's eyes. I thought of how many lies I would tell in the coming days. *It wouldn't be easy*.

After this conversation, I felt like I was splitting into two. A happy Sue with Steve, whom no one knew anything about, and another Sue with everyone else. One who had to live in lies to protect the happy Sue. Two people, neither of them completely who I was.

What if my mom met Amanda somewhere and asked her about the party? What would my mom do if she knew I was lying? I was worried, but part of me was happy I tricked my mom and wasn't telling her everything about my own life. I was not a child anymore. I could have my own life, which no one had the right to know anything about. I deserved my freedom.

That night, I was in bed, trying to think of what to tell Amanda if she asked me about my plans for the weekend, when I heard a fight between my mom and Tommy. Their fights were more frequent recently. I took a deep breath, smiled and thought that would make my life with Steve easier for sure. My mom would be busy with her own problems, and she wouldn't care about anything I do. Also, for the first time since I met him, I hoped she wouldn't break up with Tommy. His presence, with all his problems, would definitely help me now.

The cell phone rang, and I saw Amanda's name on the screen. I expected that call.

"Hey, Sue, how are you?"

"I'm doing okay."

"I miss you so much. What if we go out with John and Amy this weekend to do something fun? I just got my driver's license and I'm so excited to drive you all," she said.

"Sure. We can do that Sunday afternoon," I said.

"Why not Saturday?"

"Nothing, I just feel like I need to rest one day a week."

"Sue, I don't know what's going on with you. Are you upset because of something I did? You are treating me differently. I never see you and talk with you now. We used to talk and see each other every day. Now, you always have excuses."

"Amanda, you are my best friend. You have been since third grade and you know that you are the closest person to me. I'm not upset about anything. I just feel confused and need to take time for myself. I promise to see you more and talk with you more soon. Just give me some time."

"Fine. I just wanted to make sure you're okay."

"If you're available Sunday, we'll spend time together," I said.

"And anyway, we'll see each other on Monday."

Sarah 5
My heart and the shed

Qena, Egypt 2012

The next morning, I walked to school as usual, and was waiting to feel as if someone was following me, but it didn't happen. I finished the school day and looked at the grill spot, but Sileem was not there. I made sure not to look around for him in case he was somewhere looking at me. I acted like nothing had happened. I talked with Mariam about the new TV show we started to watch the night before, and then left to walk back home.

On my way, I acted like nothing had happened yesterday; even though my heart was beating so fast when I got closer to the spot where I met Sileem the day before. I also found myself smiling when I remembered his words to me. I wished he would stop me again, but all I did was start running back to my home.

At home, I was sad. I really wanted to see him and listen to what he wanted to say. I didn't know how to find him. But I wasn't ready to take that step. It was a big fight between my mind, which was saying *No,* and my heart, which was saying *Yes.*

The next three days passed, and he didn't show up at the school or on my way home. The days were too long and very sad. I was just hoping to see him from a distance selling corn again, but it didn't happen. I was almost sure that he disappeared because I threatened to tell my dad. Surely, he was worried about his own dad's job in case I told mine. My father would never let his dad work for us, if he knew about Sileem having followed me. I wished I hadn't said that, so at least he would keep selling the corn to help his family, and I could see him.

On the third day, I was on my way in the morning when I felt someone was following me again. I was happy it might be him. I slowed down and was hoping he would stop me as he did the last time. Right before I passed the train track, I saw something in front of me. A paper wrapped in a piece of cloth and clipped with a clothespin flew over me and landed on the ground. I looked around, and didn't find anyone but a group of little elementary school kids on the other side, laughing and joking around. They didn't notice me or the paper, which flew over me. I picked it up and waited until after the kids passed me. I stopped, and I opened it.

> *To Sarah, the most beautiful girl I have ever seen*
> *in my life. I know all I could do was to see you*
> *from faraway, and I know all I can dream of*
> *doing is to speak with you once. I also know that*
> *I would do anything and risk anything just to*
> *not lose the possibility of my dream coming true.*
> *This is a note for you with my handwriting and*
> *my name on it. You may give it to your family to*
> *punish me, or you may burn that paper when you*
> *go home and agree to see me tomorrow right after*

school on the street where I saw you the last time.
I will talk with you just once for five minutes,
and I will never bother you again.

Thank you,
Sileem Ali

For some reason, I was shaking. I couldn't believe what I just read. I knew the right thing to do was to rip up the paper and keep walking as if I didn't care about what was in it, because I was sure he was somewhere around, looking for my reaction after reading it. I smiled and kept the paper in my pocket. He still would be worried, because I might give it to my dad. I kept walking to school. The happiness in my heart made the decision for me.

The next day after school, I walked to the street that he mentioned in the letter. I crossed the street at the spot he chose and waited for a minute. I was worried, and didn't like that he wasn't waiting for me. I thought about leaving and when I decided to leave, I saw him.

"I was waiting for you on the other side," he said.

"Were you sure I would come?"

"Yes. My heart said you would come and I always believed in my heart."

"Then why did you leave me waiting if you saw me from the other side?"

"I was looking at you and wondering if you would ever wait for me," he said.

"I was leaving when you showed up."

"I saw that, and that was why I appeared," he said.

"The five minutes are almost done just talking about seeing me, and I won't stay one minute more." I was trying to act serious.

"I enjoy looking at you and talking with you anyway," he said.

"But I am here to listen to the answers to my questions and not for you to enjoy looking at me." Now I was trying to be stern.

"OK. What do you want to know?" he said.

"Why were you following me on those mornings?"

"To answer this question, I have to tell you the whole story. I always saw you as one of the princesses we've heard about in stories since we were little. I was about six years old when your aunt asked my dad to bring me to your front yard to play with you. I couldn't believe it when I stepped in your beautiful house for the first time and I was amazed by all the toys you had, but what I liked the most was that I played with the princess. My happiness didn't last long because of your dad," he stared at the ground as he was recalling the moment. "I still remember the day he came and saw us playing and I remember all the yelling and the curses to me and to my dad. And how he asked my dad to stop me from coming back to his house. It was not the only thing he did; he also forced my dad to send my mom and all of us to live at my grandmother's place. And even though it was not my dad's fault or any of ours, my whole family was separated and punished for no good reason. But I didn't care about all of that, all I cared about was that he separated me from you. I just wanted to see you again any way possible."

He looked into my eyes, then he continued, "After a couple of years, I asked my dad if I could come after school to help him. He was worried in the beginning to let me help him, but I told him that I didn't think your dad still remembered that old situation and I also told him I would do my best to not let him see me there. I would just go help my dad, and leave the next morning for school. My dad agreed, but under one condition, which was to not do it every day, just a couple of days a week. I accepted his condition and I was so happy for that, not to help my dad, but to get the chance to be close to you again and see you from far away."

I was empathetic to everything he said, and wanted him to tell me more, so I didn't say anything and he continued.

"I kept doing that and following you to school in the morning. One day I noticed you were saying something, so I got closer to hear you and I heard you singing, and then I heard you talking to yourself and saying funny things. When I got closer to hear you better, you noticed me and looked back, so I hid in the field and kept doing that every time. I didn't mean to scare you or anything. And I am sorry if I did."

"I have to go now," I uttered.

"Is it because my five minutes are done? Or because you have no other questions for me?"

"I still have questions but I can't be late. I have to go now."

"Do you want to meet again tomorrow?" he asked.

"No way. I can't see you again on any street. If I was seen by any of my dad's family or workers, I would be in big trouble, and you as well."

"Does that mean you are worried about me?"

"No. I didn't mean that." I avoided looking into his eyes.

"Sarah, wait. I need to see you again and tell you everything. I understand the situation and I still give you two options. If you come out on your balcony tonight at seven and burn the letter I gave to you, I will know that you will come to see me again safely without fear of getting caught. And if you don't show up, I will understand that you don't want to see me anymore, and I promise to not be in your way again."

I left right away without saying anything. I really wanted to ask him how I could see him again without fear, but I wasn't brave enough to ask that question. After a couple of steps, he stopped me by calling my name.

"Sarah. I know that you want to know how I could see you without fear. We could meet next to the shed in your field at 10:00 pm, when everyone would be asleep. If I see you burning the letter at 7:00 pm, I will wait for you at 10:00. I really hope to see you."

Susan 6
The first date

Illinois, USA 2012

My hair was straight and down. I wore some makeup to look beautiful and I put on my favorite dress. It was my short blue dress, which I got as a birthday gift from Amanda last year. Amanda was the only one who remembered my birthday every year. *I really miss her.*

"Where are we going?" I asked Steve, when I got into his silver BMW, a car which I have never dreamed I'd ride in on a Saturday afternoon, to spend the day and the night with my love for the first time.

"I planned everything for you. Just wait 45 minutes and you'll see."

I was so excited to be with him and it still felt like I was in a dream, not in real life.

He had my favorite hip-hop song on in the car when it stopped in front of an old house in a quiet rural area.

"Where are we?" I asked him.

"We're at my grandfather's house," he said.

"It looks old and kind of scary with no neighbors around. What if someone attacked us here? No one could save us. Especially if no one knows we both are here!"

"Really, Sue! That is what you are thinking about on our first date alone? Don't worry, babe, no one on earth can harm you when I am around. I promise to protect you with my own life. Come with me!" He stepped out of the car.

The house seemed very old, to the point I thought that Steve might break the door while trying to open it. He went into the house and held the door for me. I slowly stepped inside and then, I was completely surprised.

The place was beautiful on the inside. It was a ranch, with old furniture, but everything was so clean and neat. My favorite red and pink roses were spread everywhere around. The place smiled like a garden. Candles were everywhere. The small dining room next to the kitchen had food set out for two people.

"Wow!! This place looks beautiful," I exclaimed, walking around.

"I told you everything is planned just for you."

"When and how did you do all of that?" I asked.

"You don't need to think about anything today," he whispered "Just enjoy every second with me,"

"You know what, I never thought I was that important to you, Steve. I was thinking I was just a girlfriend you want to spend some time with and then leave."

"I am not Mark," he said.

"Did you know about Mark too? I never told you about him." I tried to avoid his eyes.

"Sue, look at me. I want you to know that I really love you, and our relationship is not just a date for a while. I know you told me everything about yourself, your mom, even what Tommy did to you, but when you told me about Mark, you didn't tell me the whole story. And it was not hard for me to find out everything about it." He said this and brought bottles of beer from the fridge.

"It was not easy to tell you he cheated on me," I said, feeling a tear deep in my heart.

"Starting today, you will not have sadness. Your life with me will be different. I will do everything I can to make you happy." He came closer, held my hands, took me to the bedroom and closed the door.

With him, I felt like I was in heaven. Steven was everything I wished for. The love, the care, and the kindness from the most handsome boy I have ever seen, just for me. After a night full of love with him, I wished that the next day wouldn't come. In the morning, I woke to see him bringing me breakfast in bed.

"You are spoiling me, Steve!"

"You are my princess, Sue. Why wouldn't I spoil you?"

"When did you buy this breakfast?"

"I had everything in the fridge ready yesterday,"
I grinned hearing his words.

"What time is it?" I ate a bite of the bagel.

"It's almost noon."

"What!!" I screamed. I got out of bed and tried to get ready to go. "I have to go now. I don't want to wait until my mom calls Amanda. Then she would know I wasn't at her house last night. Also, I have to see Amanda this afternoon like I promised her. Please, let's go back to town."

"OK, sweetheart. I'll be ready in a few minutes."

On our way back to town, Steven asked me to be with him more often and he said, if it worked this time, it should work every time without anyone knowing anything.

I asked him again to share my secret with Amanda, but he refused and seemed angry about the idea, and I really didn't want to see him not happy or unsatisfied. I would do anything I could to make him happy. He had become the most important person in my life. He became my whole life.

Sarah 6
My new life

Qena, Egypt 2013

I floated back home. He was thinking of me all those years. He followed me to school and listened to my crazy songs and words. He wished to see me and talk with me. I was joyful that someone cared for me when I thought I was lonely.

I also appreciated that he trusted me enough to give me a letter with his name, and he risked everything important in his life just to see me. I wished I could tell Mariam or my aunt about him, but I knew that was impossible. If anyone discovered his feelings toward me, it would be the end for him and his family in this village.

I wasn't sure why I was attracted to him that much, since I knew that my dad would never accept him as a husband for me. My dad hated when he played with me as a little child, so anything else was completely impossible. But I couldn't resist my feelings toward him. I really loved being with him. The days I couldn't sleep when he disappeared were a sign that I really wanted to see him. The joy I felt when he was talking to me after school was another sign that he was not a regular person to me. At that moment, I was looking at the clock, waiting for 7 o'clock to come, the letter in my hand and the lighter in the other. I couldn't wait to see him again and listen to everything he wanted to say. I really wanted to know more about him. I had never had any relationship with anyone before, or had any similar feelings towards any boy. And I just wanted to get as much as I could from the happiness I felt next to him.

At seven o'clock, I went out on my veranda and burned the letter. I was looking around, trying to find out where he was watching me from. I couldn't see him, but my heart felt him and imagined his beautiful smile, the satisfaction and the happiness he had seeing the smoke coming from the veranda, so I smiled as well.

Everyone in my house was asleep by 9:00 p.m. I got myself ready to go out the kitchen door, which would lead me to the shed in the back right away. I worried that someone might wake up while I was leaving the house and notice me. My bedroom was the only one downstairs, and that was perfect for me to leave without anyone hearing my steps. After I left, I looked up and made sure all the lights were off, then I took slow, quiet steps to the shed and sat behind it. This place was perfect; none of the house guards were on that side of the house because it had the field and a big fence too, while the front was open to the streets where people and carts passed through there. I sat on the ground behind the shed and took a deep breath waiting again for Sileem, the second time in the same day. I smiled and remembered his words that afternoon when he said he liked watching me, so I looked around and saw him staring at me.

"Really? You are here looking at me," I said.

"I spent years looking at you, so I could do it anytime and anywhere."

"I don't have much time to stay here. I can stay for a half hour. I can't take the risk of someone waking up and realizing I am not at home."

"I can't really believe you are here with me now. I was so happy when I saw you burning the letter; I came to the shed and I have been sitting here waiting since then. Also, forget about leaving before listening to everything I have to say. Only then, you can leave. And don't worry about your family. I know they all go to bed early, and you were the only one who likes to stay up late."

"How did you know that?"

"I told you I have been watching you for years, Sarah. And I used to watch you from here. Look!" He pointed to my veranda, which was visible from that spot.

"Where is your dad now?" I asked.

"My dad is sitting in the front, smoking and listening to the Radio. Away from here. Don't worry about him. Everything will be fine. I promise."

"OK, let me hear what you want to say now."

"What I really wanted to say is I love you!"

I was shocked by his words. I had a feeling that he liked me, but I didn't expect him to say those words the first time we saw each other. I felt dizzy and my heartbeats went fast. But deep in my heart, I knew what was happening was not right.

"Sileem, I appreciate your feelings but if I accept to come here and listen to you, it doesn't mean that I can have any relationship with you. I think you totally understand the situation and you know my dad would never accept that.

"Sarah. I know all of that, but the most important thing for me now is you. Forget about anything else that might affect your decision and tell me what you feel towards me."

"I can't forget everything, Sileem. You know that we live in a small village in Upper Egypt. We don't live in a city or in a modern country. Our traditions here are the most important to everyone and any relationship between us would be against these traditions. My dad wants me to marry either someone from his family or someone from the other important family in the village, and he would never accept any other one for me."

"Is it because I am the son of a poor farmer who is working as a guard for your dad that I should not let my heart love you?"

"Sileem, look at me. If it was up to me, I really don't care who you are or what your dad does. All I care about is what I feel with you."

"And that was all I needed to hear now. Tell me what you feel for me, Sarah. Please!"

"OK. I feel happy when I talk to you, and the weird thing is that I feel secure when I am next to you, despite all the fears I should feel." I noticed his beautiful smile got brighter when he looked into my eyes.

"Is it hard to say that you love me?"

"I don't really know if these feelings are the same love that I hear about in the movies or something else."

"Let me tell you, it is the same love you hear about in the movies. You know I am two years older than you and surely know more than you."

"Maybe!"

And we both laughed

"There are more things I feel with you, Sileem."

"What?'

"I feel very comfortable with you; I feel myself without any acting fake that I have to do most of the time as the mayor's daughter everywhere else. Also, I don't feel lonely with you. These were my reasons to buy corn from you every day."

"I wish you could measure the level of happiness in my heart now, Sarah. You would be surprised."

"I don't need to measure it; I think it would be the same level as mine."

We kept talking that night until it was midnight. I looked at my watch and couldn't believe the time flew by that fast.

"I have to go, it's past 12." I stood up and got ready to leave.

"OK, but I will wait for you tomorrow at the same time and the same place. Next to this shed."

And starting from that day, I had a secret life, which no one knew anything about.

Susan 7
Together forever

Illinois, USA 2013

I spent the best time of my life with Steven after our first date at his great grandfather's old house. I loved that place and hoped one day to be married and live there.

The lies to Mom and Tommy were working well, but my grades were low for the first time in my life. As usual, my mom didn't notice, and for the first time, I didn't care. Steven kept treating me like his princess, and that was enough. He filled my life with surprises, gifts, and love, though he still ignored me when we met at school.

The days passed, and we celebrated Steven's 18th birthday together in the old house, and right before the end of the school year, I had only one argument with him. When I saw him with one particular girl many times, I was so angry. It was our first fight at the old house.

"Who is she, Steve?" I yelled. "And why have you been with her a lot recently?"

"Sue, please calm down and stop yelling at me."

"I will not stop until you tell me everything now. Do you like her? Are you bored with me now and don't love me anymore? You're not cheating on me, right? Tell me now!!"

"Sue, calm down. I will explain everything to you, but you have to take a deep breath and sit here first, so we can talk." He touched my shoulder.

"Don't touch me. You have to answer my questions now."

"OK. This girl's name is Anna. She's a freshman. She is my mom's best friend's daughter. She has been asking me to help her in some classes for a while, but I was so busy with everything. I thought helping her now might be a good idea, so no one would think we are together."

"Are you kidding me, Steve? You don't want anyone to know you are dating a sophomore, so you go around with a freshman? It does not make any sense, and I'm not stupid. Tell me the truth. Tell me you like her."

"Sue, I didn't tell anyone I'm dating her. She and I are just friends."

"Just friends, and that's why she never misses any of your football games. And I see her with you around the school all the time!"

"You just said she never misses a game, but I never invited her to any of them. The only thing I do with her is help her in some of her math and science classes, when she asks for it."

"So, how do you explain that she is always following you around?"

"She might like me."

"Are you trying to drive me crazy? Why are you with a girl who you know likes you, while you're dating me?"

"By the way, you look beautiful when you are jealous, Sue!" he commented, looking at my eyes.

"Steve, don't change the subject. I told you before. I will be fine if you leave me, but don't cheat on me."

"You're answering yourself, Sue. If I didn't love you and I liked her, why am I here with you now? And why would I let you see me with her if she's not just a friend? I understand your frustration and I know it's because of your experience with Mark, but again, Sue, I am not Mark."

"But you said she likes you, and it's not OK to be with her that much if you realize that. You're opening a door for her, Steve." I said, calmer.

"I know what I'm doing. She didn't tell me she likes me and, if she would say or do anything to show that, I would never let her be my friend. Sue, I love you and can't wait to let everyone know you are my girlfriend."

"Steve, I believe you, but it is still not easy on me."

"OK, would you be happy if I wasn't around her at all?"

"Yes," I said, taking a deep breath.

"OK, but remember, I can't be away from every friend who happens to be a girl, just because you are jealous."

"I understand, and that never bothered me, except with this girl."

"Is it because she is beautiful?" he grinded, trying to tease me.

"Do you really think she is beautiful?"

"I think you are the most beautiful girl I have ever seen. You're my princess. You know, Sue, if we lived in a different state, that allowed us to marry, I would marry you now. That's how much I love you."

"I wish we lived in Massachusetts," I stated. "They allow girls to marry at 12 years old, and boys at 14. But it would still be hard to convince your parents."

Steven graduated high school, and I barely finished my sophomore year. I failed some classes, but finally, I was able to pass the school year. I was so happy that Steven was accepted into college for pre med. The dream is getting closer to being true. And soon we might be together forever as he promised.

Sarah 7
The deep hole

Qena, Egypt 2013

The best couple hours of my week were those that I spent with Sileem next to the shed in the dark nights. I finally found a reason for my life. Someone to complete me. I was sure this was the love I'd heard about in songs and movies. All I needed in this world was to be next to him for the rest of life.

On one of those nights, I was talking to him when we both heard someone yelling his name.

"Sileem, Sileem!"

"Oh my goodness!"said Sileem. It's my dad coming this way."

"What should I do now?" I asked. Then I covered my face with my scarf. At that moment, my body was shaking.

"Get inside the shed fast. Now." he said, and opened the door for me. "And be quiet."

"Yes, Dad. What do you need?" Sileem asked. When it became harder to hear their voices, I realized he was trying to lead his dad away from the shed.

"Who were you talking with?" Ali asked.

"No one!" said Sileem.

"I just heard you talking, boy. I am not too old to imagine things yet."

While I was listening to the conversation, I sat on the floor, holding my head in my hands, wishing for a hole in the ground would appear and make me disappear. I looked around the dark dirty shed. It was filled with gardening supplies, and other things I didn't recognize. I stood, and moved toward the wall, hoping to hear their voices clearly.

"I know you are not old, Dad. I was talking to a friend on my phone."

"Why are you talking to a friend this late?" Ali asked. You need to go to sleep now. It's late, and you have to help me tomorrow morning. Also, you need to sell corn again. We need that money for your sister's wedding."

"OK, Dad, I understand. I will go now."

I heard steps going far away, so I realized he took his dad and went back to his room. I wasn't sure if I should go or **stay.** Would he come back? There was no time to think about that. When I looked at my watch, I saw that it was after 1:00 a.m. already. My dad would wake up to pray the Morning Prayer in a couple of hours and I had to be in my bedroom before that.

I tried to open the shed's door, but I couldn't. I realized that Sileem had locked it. Maybe he didn't know he had locked it. I was so scared. My dad would kill me if he knew where I was at that moment and why. I didn't know what to do, so I sat back on the floor and cried. I wasn't sure how long I cried before I heard someone was opening the door. My heart almost stopped, thinking it was my dad or my brother or even Ali, but I let out a long sigh when I saw it was Sileem.

"I remembered I locked the door, so I came back," he said, and he kindly patted my back. Then I felt calm. The world was better when I felt his touch and when I looked up into his beautiful eyes.

"I was so scared. I didn't know what to do."

"It's OK now. Go back home before your dad gets up."

He interrupted me when I was walking away. "Sarah."

"Yes."

"I will wait for you tomorrow."

"No. I can't take this risk again."

"No risk. We will meet tomorrow inside the shed."

Then I left.

I made it safely to my bedroom, but I couldn't sleep at all. I asked my aunt the next morning If I could stay home from school. I told her I had stomach pain all night and didn't sleep because of it. It was my first time I ever lied to my aunt. I knew it was a big sin to lie, but I didn't know what to say other than that. I think God, whom they told me about, would understand the situation.

I hesitated to go the next night and meet Sileem in the shed. But the other option was not to meet him again, and that I surely couldn't do.

So I went on time, and saw something I didn't expect. The messy, dirty old shed looked totally different from the night before.

"Wow. What did you do here? It looks beautiful and clean."

"I did everything I could to make you happy and safe."

"But that means you didn't help your dad at work today and didn't sell corn or make any money for your sister's wedding. It seems like you wasted all the money you had on these decorations and candles," I said, looking around the place.

"This is true,"he said. I understand I have to work hard to help my family afford life, but I don't like that I have to work hard to help my sisters in their weddings. I think it is not fair for men who want to marry at a young age like me."

"So, are you really planning to marry early?" I said with a shy smile.

"Yes, as early as I can. I wish it were right now," he said, and approached me.

"Stop, are you crazy? What are you doing? Get me out of here right now," I felt scared for the first time with him.

"What is wrong? Why are you scared and angry?"

"Sileem, you know we shouldn't be together alone in a closed place. This is forbidden in Islam, and I don't want to be a sinner and go to hell."

"But you know, we can't keep meeting outside of here or we will risk a big problem. I don't care about myself, but I don't want to get you in any trouble, Sarah."

"Yes, but that shouldn't be a reason to be here now." I felt so confused.

"OK. I want you to calm down and sit here now so we can talk and I promise, I won't do anything you don't want me to do."

I sat on a yellow pillow on the floor, and he sat on a red one next to mine.

"Sarah, I want you to answer my questions first, then we can talk."

"Fine."

"Do you love me?"

"Yes."

"Do you think the time we spend together is worth the risk you take every time you come here?'

"Yes."

"Do you want to be with me for the rest of your life?"

"Yes."

"Do you agree to marry me?"

"What do you mean?"

"I mean if you love me and want to be with me forever and are not comfortable being here with me because it is a sin, we can marry and it would be halal to be together."

"But how? My dad would never accept this."

"Your dad won't know."

"How could you bring a ma'zoon to perform the marriage ceremony and my dad wouldn't know?" I said "The ma'zoon and the two witnesses would definitely tell him and all the people of the village as well."

"Sarah, listen to me, do you think when Prophet Muhammad came and established Islam, they had ma'zoons to get married and papers to sign for marriage? They had none of that. The marriage back then was just words. The groom said, 'Do you want to marry me?' and the bride said, 'yes, I want to marry you.' Then they were a husband and wife."

"Really? Was it that easy?"

"Yes. And if you think about it, that would be the best solution for us now."

"But what if my family knew about that?"

"We will be very careful. No one should know anything now, for your own safety. When I make some good money and find a good job, I would come to ask for your hand and you would put some pressure on them to accept me. Then, we would have a wedding and everyone would know we are together, and no one would know anything about our old secrets here."

I was listening to him and wishing for everything he said to come true. "I have to go now," I said.

"Why? It is still early."

"Sileem, I have to think about what you said. Please, give me some time."

"You have all the time you need, Sarah, and I will always wait for you, no matter how long, I will wait."

I went back home and decided I wouldn't see him again. After I didn't see him for a couple of days, I got sick. Headache, stomach pain, and fatigue. I barely could eat or drink anything. My stomach was upset, and my whole body was upset about what I did. I couldn't go to school or study. After a whole week, my dad took me to the doctor, who prescribed medications, but they didn't work at all. Everyone in my house was worried about me. They didn't know what was wrong with me, but I knew what was wrong. He would be my first choice in my life. I just needed him.

I decided to go to school to see him again, so I stopped at his corn grill.

"Finally, you are here! I have been waiting for you every day."

"I was sick."

"Really! Are you OK now?" He seemed worried.

"Yes, I feel better."

"Did you think about what I told you?"

"Yes. I will see you tonight in the shed at 11:00"

"I can't wait," he said with a big smile, handing me a corncob.

On that night we got married just as he had described.

Susan 8
The surprise

Illinois, USA 2013

After all the happiness with Steven and all the excitement he had filled my life with, a day came that turned my whole life upside down. I bought a test and found out I was pregnant. I thought I was careful not to let that happen, but it did. I didn't know how it happened with all my caution. I didn't know what to do or who to go to.

I felt completely lost.

I can't tell Mom, she doesn't care about me, and she can't wait until I leave the house. Having a baby now will set her off. I can't even tell Amanda, who would be upset with me for hiding all my secrets from her all that time. And I can't tell Steve, who didn't want anyone to know about us dating. I don't know what he would say or do about me being pregnant now! And I don't know if he would ever accept that.

I sat on the bathroom floor. I was holding the test with one hand and covering my mouth with the other, so no one would hear my crying. My heart was so heavy. I cried until I couldn't breathe. I wished I was dead.

Sue, stop crying. Get up. Face your problem, so you can solve it. Remember there is a girl somewhere also going through what you are going through. And you both can do it.

But how? How?

God, I don't know if You really hear me. I don't even know if You exist. People say You are powerful and can do anything You want to do. I know I have never talked with You before, but I am now. I need Your help if You can. Help me, God!

I have to do something, and the only thing I can do now is to go see Steven and tell him. At least he knows most of the story and he would get only the one big shock of me being pregnant. For my mom and Amanda, it will be many shocks for everything I would tell them. Also, Steve loves me the most. He will help me to get through this problem safely. He may tell his parents and they would not leave his baby for sure. They might like me and accept our relationship, and I would help them to keep it a secret until his dad's election is over and I turn 18.

I thought, wiped my tears and washed my face and put on a fake smile on it.

"Hey, Steven, I need you now."

"It's not the weekend, sweetie! And we didn't plan to meet today. I have classes until late."

"I know, but I really need to talk with you. I will sneak out of my house tonight when you finish your class, and I'll wait for you in the alley. And we can get back before morning."

"Do you miss me that much?"

"Yes, I do! But there is also something I need to share with you."

"Sue, are you ok? You sound upset."

"I'm OK, but I have to talk with you tonight, Steve."

"Fine, hon, I will pick you up in the alley tonight two hours after class. Be on time. I will text you when I am there."

He picked me up at midnight. when Mom and Tommy were both sound asleep. In the car he asked what was happening, but I couldn't say a word for a bit.

"Sue, what's wrong? I am really worried. You look sad and exhausted."

"I'll tell you when we are there, Steve." I tried to give myself time to think about what I should say to deliver the news.

"Did Tommy do anything to you? Did he try to touch you again? Please let me know if he did, and I know how to teach him a lesson for life,"

"It's not Tommy."

"Who is it then? Is it your mom? Or is it someone at school? I will keep you safe, Sue. Please tell me what's wrong."

"Do you love me that much? Would you ever leave me?"

"I love you so much. I will never leave you, unless you want me to," he answered

"And I don't want anything in this world more than being with you," I mumbled and my tears were running.

"Tell me now, what is wrong?" he pleaded.

"I'm pregnant."

"What? Tell me you are kidding me, please."

"No, Steve, I am not kidding. I just found out a couple of hours ago. And I really don't know how that happened with all our caution. I didn't know what to do. I needed to see you and ask you to help me."

I expected him to curse, yell at me, or even say out loud what he was thinking, but that didn't happen. He was silent the entire time until we arrived at the old house.

Sarah 8
Sins

Qena, Egypt 2013

I spent the next six months secretly going to the shed a couple of nights a week to be with Sileem, who became my husband, as I believed. I was happy whenever I was with him. He was nice, and kind. He always listened to me. I didn't need to talk to myself anymore on the way to school, and I never felt lonely since I fell in love with him. Everything was going as we planned, until that fateful day.

"Hey Sarah," said my aunt. "I need to speak with you privately."

"Yes, Auntie, just let me change first."

"No. I need to talk with you right now. You can change after we talk." Her tone of voice and manner of speaking worried me.

"Sure." I followed her to her room.

She sat on the edge of her big metal bed, and asked me to sit on the old wooden chair next to the door across from her. "Sarah, you know I love you like the daughter I never had, and I really care about you."

"Yes Auntie, I know and I love you as well, maybe more than anyone else here." I smiled to make the situation less tense.

"Ok. I got a phone call from your history teacher. She said that your grades recently have been very low. She spoke with the other teachers about you, and they all agreed that something is not right. They are concerned about the change in your grades and in your attitude. She said you always seem tired, and don't participate as you used to. What is going on?"

"I know I haven't studied as much recently." I looked down. "I am sorry for that."

"Sarah, it's not just your grades," she said, trying to look into my eyes. "I see that you've lost a lot of weight and you're not eating much at all. Is there anything you're hiding from me?"

"No. I am fine." I avoided her eyes. "I just don't feel like studying for some reason."

"And what about your dream to be a teacher? Sarah, this year is your third and last year in high school, and it is the most important of your whole life. I know your dad, brother, and grandmother won't really care if you decide to not finish school or not go to college, but you need to know that I care. You are a smart girl who could do a lot with your life. Remember, our village doesn't have enough teachers and you could help many students and people here to learn."

"Yes, but you know I wish to live in the city, not here," I said, smiling, trying to ease the tension.

"Sarah, you know what I mean. I don't care where you work, but I do care about your education and your future. I want you to be successful and to find a good person to spend your life with, and make a beautiful family. And I want you to call your first daughter Fayza, after me. Would you promise me to take better care of yourself and your school work in the coming days?"

I looked into her eyes, and wished I were brave enough to tell her everything about Sileem and myself. I opened my mouth to speak, but I remembered Sileem's words about not telling anyone now, and also the fear of separating me from him, so I held my tongue from speaking the truth.

"Okay, Auntie, I promise. But I have a question for you."

"What?"

"Is it true they didn't have to document marriage back during the time of the prophet Muhammed?"

"Yes. But there are conditions for any marriage to be halal."

"What are these conditions?"

"The acceptance for both man and woman, at least two witnesses for that acceptance, a gift from the groom to the bride, and the marriage has to be publicly known."

"What does the last condition mean?" I felt awful that I just found this out.

"Everyone around them has to know they are married," she said. "You know, adultery is a big sin in Islam, and it's important to a married couple to announce their marriage, which is the main reason for weddings. But why are you asking about that?"

"I just had a conversation with Mariam at school about that. You know she is Christian, and we were talking about the differences between our marriages and theirs, so I just wanted to check." I lied again. My life has become one sin after another.

"Thanks Auntie, I have to go now. I have a lot to do."

"Wait."

"What?"

"What were you doing last night?" she asked.

I felt my jaw stiffen, my arms trembled, and my heart beat faster. "What do you mean?" I acted like I didn't know what she was talking about, to give myself a little time to think of what to say.

"Last night, I woke up to go to the bathroom around 1:00 a.m. and I noticed a sound from the back door. I looked and saw you coming quietly inside, walking toward your room, then heard the sound of your bedroom door closing. I wanted to go downstairs to check on you, but I was so tired and I didn't want to wake up anyone else in the house, so I decided to ask you today instead."

I felt the sweat all over my body, but I had to act like there was nothing to worry about. "Last night I couldn't sleep and I was so bored. I didn't know what to do, so I decided to get some fresh air."

"But it's very cold at night and you hate the cold weather!"

"Oh yeah, that was why I came back inside right away. I couldn't handle the cold, and it was scary in the dark. Thanks, Auntie, for everything. I have to go to the bathroom now, then, I will study for a while before lunch." I left quickly to escape.

I wondered if she would make the connection between my question about marriage and me going out last night. I was afraid, but deep in my heart I knew my aunt would never make the connection because she would never imagine that I would do what I had, in fact, done.

After I left my aunt's room, I went to the bathroom feeling sick. I threw up everything in my stomach. I looked at my face in the mirror. *Would fear make me sick? Or is it the feeling of guilt? I have to stop going to the shed for a while. If my aunt sees me again, she might follow me, or ask me again, and then I might not be able to lie. I have to tell Sileem.*

I opened the bathroom door, yelled my aunt's name to help before I stumbled, and fainted.

Susan 9
The old house

Illinois, USA 2013

Steve and I arrived at the old house. For the first time, it was filled with silence and sadness. We both sat on the brown couch in the living room. Steve was looking down, pressing on his forehead like he was in pain or deep in thought. I leaned back, looking at the ceiling. My eyes were filled with tears ready to fall just as my days and my heart were falling.

"Steve, I am so sorry. You know it was not my fault, right?" I tried to get his attention and his kindness back, but he didn't respond. "Steve, please talk to me. We need to find a solution. I know it's not easy, but we have to do something."

"I know, Sue. There is just one solution for this and no other options."

"What? Is it to tell your parents?"

He kept looking at me, but didn't answer.

"Steve, please don't ask me to have an abortion. I can't kill a human being, and it's not just a human, it's our baby." I kneeled on the floor in front of him.

"It's not about the baby now. It's about you," he said, with a weird look.

"What do you mean? Are you angry with me? Steve, do you think I did this on purpose?" Then, I was sobbing.

"Did you tell anyone about our relationship?"

"No. I swear, I didn't. I kept my promise."

"Sue, come with me." He grabbed my hand and pulled me toward the basement.

"Where are we going? Please talk to me. You need to tell me what you are thinking?" I tried to pull my hand away from his tight painful grip. I was terrified.

He kept pulling me, aggressively, without looking at me. He clearly didn't care about my feelings.

He took me down to the small room in the basement, which was dark and empty, except for a wood chair, some old tools, and other random old things. He threw me roughly into the chair, and before I realized what was happening, he got a long rope from the corner of the room and started tying me.

"What are you doing?" I was in shock and couldn't believe what I was seeing. Flashes back to my dad beating up my mom came to mind.

"You need to stay here until I decide what to do," he said hysterically.

"Will you leave me here alone? I need to go back home. Steven, I have a mom and a life. I have to go home and I swear no one will know anything about my pregnancy or us. If you want me to have an abortion, I will, but please let me go, please!!" I begged him, sobbing.

"I can't let you go. If you tell anyone, my whole family and I will be in trouble," he said, making sure I was securely tied to the chair.

"Steven, what about your baby?" I tried to appeal to his fatherly emotions.

"I don't have babies. I am not sure it's mine. It might belong to Tommy."

I wasn't sure what hurt more, the tight rope around my body or his choking words around my heart. "Steven, please don't say that. I'm pregnant by you, and you can take a DNA test to make sure he is yours."

"Really, you want me to take a test so not just my family, but everyone else would know that the 18-year-old med student who is a son of a congressman raped a 16 year old girl and got her pregnant. That's what you want the world to hear about, right?" He yelled like a crazy man. "Scream as loud as you can. No one will hear you here. Don't resist. Stay here until I come back."

I was sure this madman talking to me wasn't the Steven I loved for these past months. He was different in every way. I saw hate and felt pain, instead of love, and care. I hoped I was in a nightmare and could wake up to see my loving Steven back. Steven, the one who I'd choose over anything and anyone else. I closed my eyes because I didn't want to see this person anymore. Even his face looked different to me. He was so scary, just like my dad.

I heard his steps going upstairs. He went out; I heard the door slam and the car engine. I opened my eyes and I was alone, tied in the chair in the small room in the old secluded house with no one around.

Sarah 9
My aunt

Qena, Egypt 2013

I was in a very dark place alone. Faraway, I saw my aunt, my dad, brother, and my grandmother. I could barely see them, and none of them saw me. I called them loudly to notice me but, every single time I called, they went farther away, and I felt more scared. Then, I saw another girl my age. She pointed to a spot in the dark. I touched where she pointed, and felt a light switch. I flipped it, and light was everywhere around me, but I couldn't see anyone, except my aunt. I heard all their voices around me. Their voices got louder and louder, and then I opened my eyes.

I was lying on my aunt's bed when I woke up from my dream, and I heard a lot of yelling and crying. I was alone in my room just as I had been in my dream. I wasn't sure what was happening outside my room, but I heard a lot of talking, and heard my name over and over. They seemed angry. My aunt was crying; I recognized her voice. I heard the word *die*. I felt confused and wondered if something happened to my grandmother. I hoped she didn't die. But if not that, what was happening? Why were they angry?

Sarah 9

I got out of the bed, holding the wooden chair to reach the door.

Right before I opened it, I heard the word *pregnant*. I stopped and felt like I was freezing. Now the words and the tone of their voices made more sense.

Am I pregnant? Is that why I haven't been eating well recently?Is that why I felt sick and called my aunt to help before I fainted? Do they just think that? Or am I really pregnant? Will they kill me?

All these questions attacked my mind, and I felt like my brain would explode. I looked up and said, "God I know I committed many sins. I know I have never prayed before, but I promise to stop sinning and pray to You every day. I don't even know if You hear me or not, but please if You hear me, I don't want to die now. Help me!" Then, I burst into tears.

I walked to the door to listen to what they were saying and looked through the peephole.

"We need to know who has done that first. He has to be killed as well," my dad said.

"I am not going to wait; I will kill her now!" my brother yelled "This's the worst shame that could happen to us. I can't believe Sarah did this. She has to die, now!"

"I just want you to wait, Adnan," said my aunt. "We still need to hear her side of the story."

"You need to stop talking, Fayza," my grandmother screamed at my aunt. "You spoiled her so much and this is the result. She is unmarried and pregnant by someone we don't know. I'm glad I was a midwife before I married, so I could determine her pregnancy and we didn't have to ask a doctor to check her, or the whole village would be talking about our shame now."

I saw my brother holding his rifle and coming toward the room. My aunt screamed, "Wait!! If you kill her now, everyone in the area will hear the noise, and they might see the body. And everyone in the village would talk about the shame in the mayor's house. They would guess what exactly happened. There are not many reasons for a family to kill their daughter in southern Egypt. We have to think about saving our family's honor. Remember if you kill her now, we might lose the status of mayor in the family forever."

"What should I do then, our philosopher?" my brother mocked.

"Let me talk with her to find out who did that to her, and we might bring him here and get them married," my aunt said.

"What are you talking about, Fayza?" my dad said while getting his gun ready. "That would be bad for the family as well. What if that jerk tells his family or anyone else? What if he denies that he is the father of her baby? Adnan, go kill her. I don't want to see her anymore after what she has done to us. If you don't kill her now, I will."

My body was shivering, and my tears were like endless heavy rain. *They all agreed to kill me. Where was my mind when I decided to marry Sileem? The marriage that ended up not even a true marriage. I knew our traditions very well. I knew they would kill the girl if she got pregnant without being married. Even though killing is one of the worst sins Islam. It's a bigger sin than adultery. But, I know there are no choices when it comes to the honor of the family here, but killing. They also don't give any woman her inheritance money from her dad, to keep the wealth safe from strangers of the family (their husbands), for the honor of the family. Even though that was against Islam that we follow, as well. The honor of the family always comes first here. Why did I listen to Sileem blindly, and why did I do that to myself, and my family? I don't want to die now!* These were my thoughts while sitting next to the door, on the floor crying, falling apart, and feeling completely lost.

At that moment, my aunt shouted. "Listen to me, I will tell you how to kill her without anyone finding out about it."

Even you, Auntie! It seems like no escape from death. Escape! I should try to escape. Maybe jump from the balcony? But I would never survive jumping from the second floor to the rough concrete while pregnant. I just realized I have another person in me.

I touched my belly and thought, *I won't kill you, as they want to kill me. We either live together or die together.* Just then, I felt stronger and ready to die. I looked up and said, "Allah, I am ready to get back to You and all I want from You now is to forgive all my sins. Please!"

Susan 10
The dream

Illinois, USA 2013

I was in a big maze. I could see the large bushes looming above me. I needed to get out of it but I couldn't. I kept screaming, calling for my mother, Tommy, and Amanda, but no one answered. The paths in the maze all looked similar and the sun was setting. I was so afraid and shivering from the cold. I felt like I was dying. I called out to God, pleading to Him to help me and, right after I did, I saw a spot of light shining in the dark, and I heard a voice. "Here, walk through here."

"Where are you?" I screamed "Who are you? And walk through where? Help me, please!"

I looked up to where the light appeared. I saw a girl my age lost in another maze similar to where I was. She was crying, then she started running to the right, then the left, then straight following the light. I did exactly what she was doing, right, then left, then straight. After I did that, I saw my mom was waiting for me at the other end with open arms and a big smile. She gave me the hug I had always craved. The spot of light got brighter like the sun and it was in my eyes, preventing me from seeing. When I finally was able to open my eyes, I was in the chair, trapped in the old house. And the sunlight was coming in from the small window at the top of the basement wall shining right in my eyes.

I didn't know how long I had slept. Maybe a couple of hours. I thought about the dream for a minute. *What did that mean? Who was that girl, and how could I get out of here?*

I was so afraid, and confused. I didn't know what to do. I wondered if my mom would notice my absence and call the police. I also wondered how they would find me.

I had to do something. I tried to move the chair to the window, but I couldn't. I kept trying until the chair fell on its side. It was painful, but the feeling of failing my love was more painful. I needed to untie myself first before doing anything else. When I fell, I thought about moving with my shoulder and the side of my leg on the floor. There was a small sharp metal object on the floor next to a toolbox under a small table in the room. I was full of hope when I saw it. If I reached it, I could use it to untie myself and get out.

I felt as if hot shards of glass were moving through my blood. The effort I made and the pain I suffered to move about five feet to reach it were more than I ever imagined. Finally, I got there. I was lucky that Steven tied my hand to the front of the chair, not the back, so I was able to reach it. While in this hard position on my side, I kept trying to cut the rope. I noticed I had to move, left, right, then straight to reach the sharp metal object, and I remembered the dream.

I kept working on cutting the rope with the piece of metal, and resting for a little bit, then working again, until I was able to free both hands. I untied my legs and finally stood. I was physically and emotionally in pain, but I had to do something before Steven came back. He locked me in the room, so I had to find a way out.

I looked up and saw the small window that had woken me up, then I remembered the dream again. I remembered the spot of light that I followed to get out of the maze in my dream. I looked up at the window and talked to God. "Do You really hear me?"

I needed something to break the window. I noticed the wooden table. I was tired, but fortunately the table was so old and rickety. I was able to break it easily after smacking it against the floor a couple times.

I stood on the chair to reach the window. I opened it. But it was too small to get my whole body through. I had no choice but to try. Maybe someone would hear or see me out there. As soon as I started to hit the screen to break it, I heard the engine of the car in the front.

I was confused. What should I do? If he found out I was trying to escape he would surely kill me. I thought he would come to the basement right away; I also thought he would never think that I was able to untie myself. I had to take advantage of surprising him. I got the plan ready. *Either I will do it right and get out of here, or I will fail and die*, I thought.

I held the table's leg and hid behind the door. As Steven came into the room with food and water in his hands, I hit him hard on the back of his head, with all the strength I could muster in my fear of death. I looked at him down on the floor and I cried. I didn't know how that evil guy could've been my beloved just one day ago. I suddenly remembered I had to leave fast, before he could get up. I ran quickly out of the room and out of the house to the street.

I couldn't believe I was finally out.

And outside, I was lost again.

Sarah 10
The train

Qena, Egypt 2013

The door opened, my brother, my dad, my grandmother, and my aunt came inside. I couldn't say a word. My brother pulled me up roughly from the floor. I saw what seemed like a fire in his eyes. He slapped my face hard and yelled. "Who did that, you whore? Tell me, so I can kill him, as I will kill you."

I didn't say a word, I didn't even cry. I would never tell them his name. I would never be the reason for Sileem's death.

"I want to kill you with my own hands," he said, "to avenge our family's honor that you ruined, but what Fayza said is the best way to save what's left of the good name of our family."

What did she say?How would they kill me? It didn't matter how, if it was going to happen anyway.

"What time is it, Fayza?" my dad asked.

"It's 2:20," my aunt replied.

"What time do you think is the best?" my dad said.

"I think 6:00 would be good," she responded.

I couldn't believe what I was hearing! My aunt, who tried a little bit ago to convince them not to kill me, now with her face set in determination, is helping them decide how to kill me. She didn't cry or even look sad.

She is one of them, and her education and love for me are not enough to forget her culture.

She didn't ask me anything or even look into my eyes.

"I can't believe you did that to us, Sarah!" my aunt cried. "We gave you everything any girl could ask for, but you just brought us all down." She yelled and slapped me in the face hard.

I was in complete shock. I wished anyone but my aunt said that and had slapped me. She had never hurt me before. I wished I had already died. Just then, my tears wouldn't stop falling.

I saw my aunt open the closet and search desperately for something. Everyone else was waiting for her. I wanted to ask what she was looking for, but I couldn't say a word. I was quietly waiting to see how they'd decided to kill me.

Finally, she found what she was looking for, a new set of my school uniform. She told me a couple days ago that she bought it for me. I couldn't understand what they were trying to do and I was wondering, *Why did she need my uniform?* I couldn't ask or guess.

My aunt started dressing me in my school uniform without a word. I couldn't stop my tears. I could hardly see her. She seemed a lot like how I had seen her in my dream.

After she finished dressing me, she pushed me onto the bed without looking in my eyes. Then she said, "She is ready now, Adnan."

Adnan had a big rope in his hand. I saw hate and anger in his eyes. I was not too scared until I looked him in the eye. He had never been too kind to me, but I never thought he would hate me this much. He tied me roughly with the rope, and for the first time I cried out loud, as if the pain from the tying let out all my heart's pain.

How had I loved all of these people, how had I thought they loved me, how were we called a family?

"Are you crying now?" my dad screamed at me, "are you afraid? But you were not afraid when you were in someone's embrace and having fun with him. You forgot everything about your family, your culture and your religion. Do you think you're one of the Western girls whom you like to watch in the movies? Stop crying so loudly. I don't want anyone to hear you. Stop causing shame." He got a big piece of duct tape and covered my mouth. Then he kept punching and slapping me while I was tied. With my mouth taped, I wasn't not even able to scream in my pain.

I was so tired from crying and the pain, I almost passed out. I didn't feel anything until I heard them talking again. I was listening to them, but didn't open my eyes.

"It's 5:00 now, are you ready?" said my dad.

"Yes. I am," said my brother.

My brother carried me and put me in a big bag, like the ones they use for transporting corpses to the city, and he closed it. I could hardly breathe. I wanted to scream, but instead my tears streamed down my cheeks. I didn't know where he was taking me but, at that point,

I didn't want to know anything. I wanted to die and be done with this hell forever.

He carried me to the car, put me inside it and drove. He stopped the car after a few minutes. He lifted me to his shoulders. I heard his heavy breathing and wished I was not able to hear at that moment. He held me and put me down on a hard surface. I felt something hard under my back, but I didn't know where I was until he said, "I wish I was doing it with my bare hands, but the train will do it for me."

I was on the train track!

He took me out of the bag, took the tape off my mouth, cut the rope off my body, but left one around my hands and one around my feet. And before I could say anything, he said "I hope you see the train coming toward you before it smashes your body, because you deserve that fear for the shame you've brought upon all of us for the rest of our lives. Go to hell, Sarah." Then I didn't see anything.

He knocked me out by hitting my head hard on the ground. I don't know how long I was knocked out, but when I opened my eyes, I looked all around. I screamed for help but no one was around. I was terrified.

I hoped someone would pass by and notice me before the train came, but I wasn't on the route to any place in the village. I was in the middle of nowhere, on the backside of the fields. There was no way someone would pass through here and see me. They picked the right spot to kill me. They would say the train hit me when I was going to school. No one would suspect that they killed me on the train track. Especially with their power in the village.

I looked up to the clear sky and saw the sun was coming up in a beautiful color with a few clouds in different shapes. *Ya Allah, please help me. I am tied to the ground, hopeless, but I know you are all powerful. Please!*

Right after I prayed, I heard the sound of the train coming. I tried to shake myself free as the last try before death, but could not move an inch, so I closed my eyes and waited to die. The sound got closer and closer.

Was that the reason I always hated the sound of the train? Is it because it would kill me?

The sound was next to my ears, and the ground was shaking from the power of the train coming closer to me. When it was its loudest, it faded until it disappeared. I opened my eyes and saw the train passing on the other side in front of me. *I am still alive! I am not dead yet! Is that a hope or more waiting and more pain?* I looked to the sky.

I looked to the right and to the left, hoping for anyone to pass this way and see me before the train came on my side. I saw from the right side someone running towards me. I couldn't tell if it was a male or a female, but it seemed to be a man approaching me. *Is it true or am I dreaming? Is it Sileem? Did he know about what happened to me and came to save me?*

The person came closer, and stood, panting, next to me. The person was wearing a Galabya, a long dress for males in our culture and Emama, a turban for males as well. His face was covered with the rest of the turban scarf.

"I am here to help you, Sarah!"

Hearing these words, I was shocked.

It was my aunt. She took the scarf off her face, and I saw her warm smile again. I felt reborn. She was holding a big pair of scissors in her hand and quickly started cutting the ropes. In a couple of minutes, she was pulling me away from the train track. She gave me a big hug, and said, "I had to do everything I did to save your life, Sarah. Try to find a place to stay and call me on my cell phone every day at midnight to keep me updated with everything happening with you. Take these and run now as fast as you can." She gave me a small piece of paper with her phone number written on it and some money.

I took them and ran, and after a couple of steps, she called me.

"Sarah, wait!!"

"Yes, Auntie." I stopped and turned her way.

"Who was the man who did that?"

"Sileem Ali." I said, looking down.

"OK, keep running, and remember, if you seek Allah, He will always be with you."

I ran, and didn't know where I was going. I just had to get out of the village as soon as I could. I can't remember how long I ran. But I realized the sun was going down. I looked around and found that I was in a different place than our village. Just when I stopped running, I felt so tired and so hungry. I bought a sandwich from a small food cart. I sat on the side of a narrow street to eat and rest. All was darkness, and the fear started to come into my heart again. *What if a gangster or an addict attacked me? Where would I go?*

I looked to the sky again. *Thank you for saving me from death. Please help me from being lost.*

I leaned my head on the wall next to me and didn't feel anything until I woke up to someone's talking.

"Hey you, girl! Are you okay? Are you lost? Do you need any help?" I opened my eyes and saw an old man wearing a religious outfit. I realized he was an Imam.

"Yes. Please I need help, for the sake of Allah," I said. I felt so comfortable when I saw him.

"Do you need money?" he asked.

"No. I need a place to stay."

"You look young, and you are wearing a school uniform. Where are you from, and where is your family?"

"I am from a different village. My family was trying to kill me and I escaped. Please help me!" I said, crying.

"Calm down. Come inside the mosque and tell me your story, and I promise to help you," he said in a kind voice.

Susan 11
The light

Illinois, USA 2013-2019

I wasn't sure where to go, but I knew I couldn't go back home. The first place that came to my mind was Amanda's house. She would help me figure out what would be the best thing to do. I knocked on her door, and her mom opened it.

"Susan, are you OK? What's wrong?" Amanda's mom said.

"Please let me in, and I will tell you everything," I said, exhausted.

"Come in."

"Is Amanda here?"

"Not yet, she should be back from school soon. Tell me what is going on, I am so worried to see you like this, Sue."

"I am OK now. All I really need is something to eat and drink. Could I have you bring me some food and water, please?"

"Sure, dear. I will. Rest on the couch, and I will bring you something to eat."

I enjoyed the sandwich she brought, and drank like I had been in the desert for days. When I finished my food, it was almost 2:15 p.m., and Amanda came home from school.

"Sue, what are you doing here?" said Amanda "Are you OK?"

"Amanda!" I hugged her, and my tears poured out on her shoulder, like a baby's.

"Sue, tell me what's going on? Why are you crying?"

"First tell me, did my mom call you to ask if I slept over at your house?"

"No, she didn't call. You didn't spend the night at your house? Where have you been?"

"Amanda, before I tell you anything I have to say I'm sorry. There is so much I have to tell you now that you don't know about me. And I was wrong in everything I have done. Please forgive me and help me!" I wiped my tears and took a deep breath to tell her the whole story.

I spent about an hour telling Amanda and her mom everything that had happened in the past ten months, since I started dating Steven in secret and until I arrived at their house.

"I knew something was wrong with you," Amanda said. "I thought you didn't like me anymore or found another friend who took my place in your heart."

"No, Amanda, you are my only friend. It hurt me to be away from you. I really missed you."

She embraced me. "And what will you do now?" Amanda asked.

"I don't know. I came to you because I need to talk with someone I trust."

"I think you should tell your mom," advised Amanda. "Go to the police and report everything that happened. I can't even imagine all these terrible things that Steven did to you. He always seemed very gentle and refined. What he did to you revealed his true self. He should be in jail now. The jail was made for people like him."

"I agree with everything Amanda said," Amanda's mom said. "You have to do that as soon as possible, before he tries to find you."

When she said that, I realized that he might come to find me at Amanda's house. "I am so worried. He might come here trying to find me. I don't think my blow to his head will keep him unconscious for long." A cold shiver ran down my spine.

"Calm down, Sue, he would never come here," said Amanda's mom. "He is probably hiding somewhere now. I think he is more afraid than you. Believe me. He knows very well what is waiting for him." Her words helped me to calm down.

"OK. Listen, I don't want to go back home," I said. "I can't face my mom with my pregnancy now. She always wished I'd leave the house and said that many times. She can barely afford paying for herself and Tommy. I have to leave this town and find a job somewhere else."

"But you have to tell your mom that you are leaving," said Amanda's mom.

"I will, but not right now."

"And what about Steven? You have to report him," said Amanda.

"I can't."

"What? Why can't you?"

"Steven did all of that out of fear of the reaction of his family. If they knew I was the reason their only son was put in jail, they would never leave my baby or me alone," I said. "They might send someone to kill me. And you know, Amanda; I won't have money to get a lawyer to help me. A step like that needs time, money, and a good plan, and I don't have any of that now. If you really want to help me, please find me a place to hide as soon as possible."

"I know someone who can help you," said Amanda's mom.

"Who?" I asked.

"My aunt Laura. She is an older lady who owns a motel in Springfield," Amanda's mom said. "She is kind, and she has been living in the motel for the past twelve years, since the death of her husband. She never had kids. I think she can help. I will call her now. I'll tell her your story, and ask if she will help you."

"Please do!"

Amanda's mom called her aunt who agreed to give me a job at her motel and a room to stay there. And that was all I needed.

"Sue, your mom may call the police when she finds out you left, and you're not answering your phone."

"She would call you first to check about me, when she finds out I didn't sleep at home last night. Let's wait and see when that happens," I dejectedly responded.

"What do you want me to tell her?" Amanda asked.

"When she calls you, give her the motel phone number, and I will take care of everything else."

"OK. You need to rest here tonight, and leave for Springfield in the morning," said Amanda. "Since tomorrow is Saturday, I will go with you to make sure you get settled there. I know you will love Auntie Laura. She is one of my favorite people."

"I don't know how I could ever thank you for all you have done for me." I said in tears. "I know I don't have a good family, but I feel I've been blessed with you in my life. Thank you!"

I rode the bus with Amanda for three hours to Springfield. And there I met Laura. She was a small, fair skinned woman in her seventies with short gray hair and an old pair of glasses. She welcomed me with a big smile, hugged me, and showed me my room in the motel. She said, "You look very tired. I made you some tomato soup and a grilled cheese sandwich. It's in your room. Eat and rest, and I will tell you about your job tomorrow."

Amanda left after I promised I'd call her as soon as I get a phone and I'd keep in touch. I entered the room and closed the door. It was a small, clean room with nice classic old brown furniture. I couldn't believe I was safe in a nice place. The past two days felt like years. It was a long nightmare that I couldn't believe was over. I hoped it was over forever. I closed my eyes and slept like I was escaping from this life to another one.

The next morning, when I woke, I remembered that my mom didn't realize my absence yet. I remembered my school, which I'd left, and my dreams for the future, which I was losing. And I cried. I cried like I had never cried before.

I really don't know why You created me, God. If You can hear me now, tell me why. Did You make me to be alone? A 16-year-old single mom living with a baby by herself, with no family, and with the fear of death every second. Why has all of this happened to me? Why?

At that moment, someone was knocking at the door.

"Who is it?" I asked.

"It's me, Laura. Susan, get yourself ready. It's Sunday morning, and I am going to church. Get ready and come with me."

I walked to the window, looked to the sky. I said, "I'm   coming."

****

Now, six years after that day, I am living in a beautiful house in Springfield with my amazing husband Martin, who is the manager of the motel, with my 5-years-old daughter Emily. Right before I started writing my story, I was sitting in my living room, getting my assignment done for my last semester in college. I'm graduating with a BA in Journalism. I achieved everything I wished for with the help of Laura, who loved me, and treated me like her daughter. And with the support I had from my husband Martin, who loved me and my daughter like his own. And my faith in God is the main reason, above all else for everything I achieved.

I'm doing all I can to give my daughter everything I missed in my life and I'm planning to teach her everything I learned. But, deep in my heart, I know that she has to live through her own mistakes and to learn her own lessons. The lessons she needs to survive her own life. I visit my mom on holidays, and she comes to visit us a couple times each year. She's suffering from depression again after she saw Tommy in an affair with another woman in her own bedroom a couple of years ago. After she broke up with him, I offered for her to come and live close to me, but she refused. The good news is that she promised to rethink that decision. It was hard to forgive my mom and Steven, but my faith helped me. Steven got himself in many troubles with other young girls, and he was arrested. I've heard he was diagnosed as a psychopath, and I wasn't surprised.

I live in peace now that I forgave them, and because every question I asked of God was answered in my life.

Susan M
Springfield, USA
On Feb 7, 2019

Sarah 11
A new world

Cairo, Egypt 2019

Sheikh Muhammad was the answer to every prayer I asked God for. He accepted me, taught me, and changed my life to a real life after it was full of fear and insecurity.

He found me a place next to his house. After the birth of my son Adam, he and his kind wife took care of me and my son. Adam, who survived everything I went through, brings me such joy. Sheikh Muhammad helped me repent to God and promise Him I would never choose to sin, because every sin leads to much pain in this life and in the hereafter. And every good deed protects and promises happiness in both worlds. He taught me to pray five times a day, and fast every Ramadan because I love my God and not because I have too. I wore my hijab because I wanted to, not because everyone around me was wearing it. He taught me these worships should help me to be a better person every day. Connect to my God, learn, improve and treat all Allah's creations with love and peace. I found my heart and the purpose of my life in that new place.

Sheikh Muhammad explained to me that what my family wanted to do by killing me and my baby was a much worse sin than mine, because killing is the worst sin, after disbelieving in God, as God told us in the Quran. He told me that culture sometimes makes people forget about their beliefs and leads them to do the opposite of what God created them for. He explained that not all the families in Egypt would have the same reaction to my mistake like my family but it's more common in the south of Egypt. He also told me how important it is to forgive my family from my heart to be able to be happy and release my pain. He taught me how to give and forgive.

****

As my aunt asked, I contacted her as soon as I found a place. She was able to visit me once in a while without anyone from the family knowing. Because, if they knew where I was, they would send someone to kill me.

For almost two years I lived a couple of hours away from my family, but I felt like I was in a different world. My aunt told me that she reached out to Sileem after I escaped and told him about what happened to me. What he said to her was the last pain my heart received from him.

"I did what I did to take my revenge out on her arrogant father who kicked me out of the front

yard for playing with her. I never hated anyone in my life more than her father and all his family. You always treated us as servants just because of your money and power, but now I can tell the whole city about what happened between me and Sarah and put your family in shame for the rest of life. Plus, I can make her father lose his position as mayor."

I couldn't believe all that I thought was love from him was actually hate. And I still can't understand what made him use me to take revenge on my father.

But the Sheikh and his wife helped me to heal from all my pain. They helped me finish my school and attend a college in the city to study history. I owe them so much.

My aunt told me recently that Saleem died in a car accident. The only thing that came to my mind when I heard that was thank Gad, I'll never see him again.

At college I met Yusuf. He was a Muslim from Indonesia, studying at Al-Azhar University in Cairo and working there. He was visiting a friend in the town where I lived. He's one more gift from God. We liked each other. I told him my story, and he didn't care about everything that had happened to me. He loved me and we got married. He also loved my son Adam and treated him as his own son. This is something that would not happen with any Egyptian man that I have ever known. No Egyptian man would accept me as a wife with my past. I don't know if they think they know better than God, who accepted my repentance the second it was happening in my heart? But my kind God sent me Yusuf, and he was enough. After a year of marriage, we moved to Cairo. Soon, it will be our fourth wedding anniversary.

I am working now as a history teacher. We go to visit Sheikh Muhammad and his wife, and my aunt comes to visit us and play with my son when she can. We'll move to Indonesia as soon as possible, because my aunt told me my family is still looking for me. It'll be safer to live and raise my son there.

I am so happy to share my story here in this private Facebook group "Survival girls" and I want also to share that I enjoyed a story I read a couple of days ago from the U.S.A which was written by a lady called "Susan M." Thank you for sharing, and I wish we could see each other one day and be friends, Susan.

Sarah A
Cairo, Egypt
Feb 10, 2019

A note from the author

This novel and its characters do not aim to represent all or even the majority of people within each culture. I drew inspiration from real stories to craft Susan and Sarah, using my imagination for every detail. I sincerely hope you enjoyed the story, and I appreciate your time in reading it. Thank you.

Rania Zeithar
12/16/2023

Acknowledgements

I dedicate this book to the Plano, IL Writers' Group for inspiring the author within me with their incredible assistance and boundless compassion. Thank you from the bottom of my heart to these amazing people for assisting me in realizing the dream of publishing my first fiction book, which is my second book in English and my third book overall:

Jeanne Valentine	Paul Block
Shalley Wakeman	Pat Comer
Glen Heefner	Patrick Helmers
Carl Armstrong	Arlene Salamendra
David Dean	Alyse Plattos
Vivian Wright	Rebecca McNabb
Laurie Stephans	Ron McDonough

Thanks, also to the following coworkers and friends for their tireless proofreading:

Hend Eldesouky	Rama Dannoura
Samantha Peruski	Noureldeen Mohamed
Delaney Rogers	

Finally, my special thanks to the cover illustrator Dana Omar and the cover graphic designer Huda Muhammed. Yusuf Faidalah and Walid Faidalah for helping in edits.